The Curse of the Snake God

The Curse of the Snake God

R. Chetwynd-Hayes

**INNER
CIRCLE**

This edition first published in
Great Britain in 1991 by
Inner Circle Books of London W1

ISBN 0-85018-087-3

Printed and bound in Great Britain by
Billing & Sons Ltd, Worcester.

Contents

I
The World We Know

CHAPTER ONE

Gentlemen, I must be allowed to make this statement in my own way, just as though I were composing it on a typewriter instead of talking into a microphone. As you must know, up to a little while ago my secondary profession was that of author and I have long ago got into the habit of thinking in sentences and paragraphs, to say nothing of chapters.

So please, gentlemen, no interruptions. Once the line of thought is broken I am apt to say the first thing that comes into my head, be it true or otherwise. And I must tell the truth, even if it is not believed – which is a certainty – for you who represent the public at large must be warned of what to expect from now on.

I must also be painfully honest, otherwise I'll be deceiving myself and that would be fatal, for it is so simple to allow imagination to paper over the cracks time has scored on the wall of memory. So to begin: I was a professional writer earning a low income. I made up the deficiency by living off women.

Be so kind, sir, as to remove that sneer from your face. I fully admit to being a gigolo; and I see nothing wrong in hiring out my assets, swopping satisfaction for money. Making two people happy: me and my client. I got quite an amount of assignments by recommendations. A few new clients from the big hotels. I bumped into Princess Helena Landi in the foyer of the Grand Palace.

Honestly. I wasn't looking for a pick-up, merely making my way to the bar for a drink, when wham – I was clutching a tallish, pale-faced, thin woman of forty or more, elegantly dressed and staring at me with large brown eyes. I said:

'I do beg your pardon. Most careless of me.'

Her English was perfect with just a hint of a mid-European accent.

'Not at all. My thoughts were miles and years away.'

I raised the flag and lowered the drawbridge. Maybe I wasn't looking for business but I had no intention of ignoring it when it came my way. She wore a short polka-dot dress and this permitted me to touch her arm, slide my fingers up to her right shoulder and take full note of the quiver that made her right hand tremble. I also noticed that the left hand was enhanced by a diamond that must have left a deep crater when it was dug up and now dazzled the eye and stirred the greed whenever the owner moved her third finger. A red ruby did nothing to distract from the beauty of the right hand which meant that the cash register that nature with a little help from me has installed in my brain, rang a sweet peal that forecast a healthy sheen to my bank account.

I said, in the right tone of voice, deep, vibrant, ear-caressing: 'Will Madam permit me to supply a restorative in the form of a champagne cocktail?'

As I had supposed, she accepted the invitation, drank two champagne cocktails – Napoleon brandy poured over a knob of sugar, then a full measure of pink champagne. I know of no better stimulant so guaranteed to arouse the bodily juices, unless it be a stone wall – four fingers of bourbon poured over chipped ice then fill up with sweet cider.

The barman and I have done business before and he, acting on a nod from me, was a bit heavy-handed when pouring the brandy in her glass and in no time I was steering her towards a small table that lurked behind a tall potted plant.

Here I examined her at my leisure.

I had dealt with worse, far worse; weighed down by fat, with boobs that were quite capable of smothering or knocking you senseless if you got in the way of an excited swing. To say nothing of thunder thighs that could break a man's back when the pressure was on. No . . . no . . . give justice where it was due she had a figure that did things to my essentials, plus really beautiful hands and arms. The face had been beautiful, but time, possibly illness or too much living had scored lines, pouched the rather splendid dark eyes and more than likely added years to her actual age – or so I thought at the time.

But the auburn wig! I had to fault her there. Far too heavy and large. A mass of curls that not only covered the scalp but hid the ears and the top half of the forehead as well. It must have been very uncomfortable to wear. But there was always the chance I might be able to chat her into doing something about her own hair – always supposing she had any. In the past I had done many a renovation job by urging the use of dye, assisting nature with false hair rammed home in the right places. If one has to work with second class material there's no reason why it shouldn't be made as attractive as possible.

In the meanwhile she was studying me with a certain rather disconcerting shrewdness, although I had no reason to suppose my appearance was anything but prepossessing. I was about to introduce myself, stress the loneliness and lack of cash that were making my life an agonizing journey, when she spoke with that clear, slightly accented voice:

'I am the Princess Helena Landi. For your information, my age is a matter for deep conjecture, my wealth unlimited and up to this moment I have been excessively bored. I am looking to you to alleviate that state.'

I pretended not to understand, put on a pretty display of confused innocence.

'I am sorry, madam, I do not understand. . .'

She laughed softly and I had to assume the splendid white teeth were the set provided by nature. 'Come, come. You wear your profession like a girl flaunting a new dress. That so pretty face, beautiful appealing eyes, the well-groomed hair – the curls I like them – the well-washed – well-shaved – well combed – and the well-brushed-looked-after-teeth. There again, you do not walk but flow. Yes, I like the way you walk.'

I could not decide if I was being complimented or mocked, so continued to look confused, ready at any moment to put on a display that would suggest hurt feelings. She laughed again and shook her head in mock reproof.

'Please, let us not play act. You are young and pretty and need money. I am not so young or very pretty and have very large amounts of money. I will enjoy your youth and beauty, you will enjoy some of my money. I see nothing wrong with that. We but follow the time-hallowed trail of commerce. You are the seller, I am the buyer.' She shrugged. 'What could be more simple?'

I have had to deal with many bizarre situations during my professional life and few have floored me, although I must confess to being very badly shaken when an American lady dispensed with all preliminaries by stating: 'If you've got some dick to sell, Honey, let's have a look at it and stop assing about.' But this direct approach did rather take my breath away, for there are civilized lines of procedure and I am of the opinion it behoves both parties to follow them. However the lady was, all said and done, the customer, who according to tradition is always right, so I merely bowed my head and murmured: 'I must compliment madam on her refreshing candour. May I enquire what she proposes?'

She again bared those splendid teeth. 'Can it be I have hurt your feelings by being a trifle too direct? Or is this a pretence you put on for my entertainment? I hope so. This is what I propose, as you so aptly put it. You will act as my social secretary and devote yourself to making me happy. Smooth my days, enrich my nights.'

'That will be a pleasure, madam.'

'If you say so. In return you will receive a cash payment of two hundred pounds per week, plus the usual presents – gold cigarette case, cuff links, whatever clothes that are necessary. All this is agreeable to you?'

I reached out for her hand but she drew it away.

'Perfectly, madam.'

'You may call me Helena in private, Madame the Princess in public. Or merely Madame. It is a non-royal title. This is understood?'

'You are the soul of clarity.'

'That is my intention. Now, I have a suite on the top floor of this hotel. The Imperial Suite. You will now accompany me there and I will introduce you to my maid. My close confidant.'

I felt much as a man who has lost control of a runaway vehicle and can only wait to see where he will finish up. So I now rose and followed my newly-acquired client to the lift, there to stand beside her until we reached the top floor, where the doors slid open to reveal a thickly carpeted hallway that was surrounded on three sides by white and gold painted doors. The liftman bowed.

'The Imperial Suite, Madame.'

The princess smiled gently. 'Yes, I know. I've lived here for the past three weeks.'

The central door opened and a striking-looking woman emerged from the room beyond. Tall with skin that looked as if it had been treated ineptly with some kind of black dye, for there were patches more dark than others, deep-set black eyes and a large nose that resembled a beak more than anything else, not enhanced by lips that were so thin as to be well nigh invisible. She performed a rather perfunctory curtsey and asked in a slightly less perfect English than that favoured by her employer:

'You have returned, Madame the Princess?'

The princess peeled off black lace gloves and tossed them on to a chair, an action that seemed to be an outward expression of her personality. 'That is obvious, is it not? This is. . .' she turned to me and asked with slightly raised eyebrows, 'the name by which you wish to be known? What is it?'

I allowed a hint of steel to enter my voice when I answered.

'My name *is* Gore Stephen Sinclair, a name that has been hallowed by time and tradition. Friends address me by my given name – Gore.'

She shook her head with playful impatience. 'I do not like that. It makes me think of blood. I will call you Chu-Chu. You look Chu-Chu. Gredelsa, this is Chu-Chu Sinclair. Perhaps he would like you to call him Mr Sinclair.'

I thought for a moment the woman was going to spit.

'I will call him nothing. Like me he is employed, but not for a purpose that does him credit.'

The princess erupted into a tirade, speaking some foreign language that could have been Italian or Greek and Gredelsa answered her with an anger that matched her own. Eventually the maid went back to the room from which she had emerged leaving her employer to shrug and mutter to herself before turning to me as her expression slowly changed, suggesting a blend of mockery and compassion. Then she said abruptly:

'Follow me and I will conduct you to your room. You may spend the rest of the day settling in.'

I began to protest for I could not subdue a feeling that she was taking me over, relegating me to the role of live-in servant, whereas I had always regarded myself as a consultant engaged to render a highly skilled service. In any case I had a very nice little flat in the region of Curzon Street where I could retire when the stress became unbearable. But the princess dismissed my objections with an imperious wave of her hand.

'Nonsense. I will require you to be on hand at all times. The very idea of your departing at sunset, or sunrise for that matter, is not to be considered. And you are a servant. A highly placed one possibly, but a servant for all that. By the way, I am not taken by what you are wearing. Much too dark, lacking colour.'

'Madam, for your information I am dressed by Norman of Jermyn Street.'

'It matters not if you have been dressed or undressed by the royal tailor, you look too English. Subdued, well-attired for a high-class funeral. I will expect to see you in a light-blue suit in the near future. And a red flowing tie I think – and yes – mauve, green and pink shirts. And do not make faces at me. I pay good money for the merchandise and therefore am entitled to chose the wrapping.' She led me to a door at the very end of the hall and after opening it preceded me into the room beyond.

It was the usual luxuriously-appointed room that is part and parcel of a suite in an expensive West End hotel. An immense bed, two great silver-pine veneered wardrobes, then a wide expanse furnished with a walnut table, matching chairs arrayed in front of a gigantic television set. I said ironically – or so I intended – 'Very nice!'

She shrugged. 'It will do. But soon we will move down to my house in the country. There we will have room to spare.'

'In the meanwhile?'

'In the meanwhile Gredelsa will give you some money. An advance on your salary – or maybe not. Depending if you are a good boy. You will be allowed fifty pounds a week petty cash, to dispense as tips to doormen, paying for taxis and so forth. If it is not enough let me know. Kindly escort me down to the restaurant at eight; otherwise the time is yours to spend as you wish.'

She extended her left hand which it was a pleasure to kiss, then left me alone in that preposterous room, feeling depressed as never before in my life, but not knowing why. On reflection, it would seem as if a once familiar fear was being reborn, proving my often repeated contention that man's immortal ego has been subjected to every experience that circumstances or fate has created. Yes, gentlemen, you may well ask how a contemptible gigolo has the gall to come out with such a profundity. Well, sirs, may I be permitted to put it to you that the least among us may well be a god in the making.

But to continue. Presently Gredelsa without bothering even to tap on the door, entered my room and flung a wad of bank notes down on the bed, then departed without speaking a single word. This was not unusual. Servants, especially those who had established a close relationship with their employer, resented my very presence and came to hate me with a spine-chilling intensity. To this day I am certain that one ancient lady's maid tried to poison me.

But money was always the great comforter and the two hundred pounds that I presently tucked into my money belt, to be removed only when in bed or the bath, did much to console me, promising, as it did, more to come.

Then having washed my face and hands, combed my hair and ensured there was sufficient money in my wallet for the payments I must make, left the suite (the grim-faced maid watching from a slightly open door) and went down to the lower regions. Down below I knew whom to interview.

The chambermaid was careful not to look at the twenty pound note and murmured: 'Pearl necklace in the safe worth the best part of thirty thousand if not more. Has a hundred thousand on a Special Reserve Account with Lloyds. A handful of credit cards. You're on to a good thing.'

'Anyone else in my line?' I asked.

The woman shook her head. 'Not now. There was a one night stand – no pun intended – around two weeks ago, but he flew the nest early next morning. Charlie, who was on desk duty, said he looked as if he'd looked into a dark room and not liked what he'd seen. Left a night bag behind, not been back for it.'

I frowned for experience had taught me that in this game there are quite a number of reasons why a man should take to the high road scared out of his naturals. I asked:

'Any idea what upset him?'

She grimaced. 'Lots of ideas, but no proof, unless it be. . .'

During the ensuing pause I peeled off another note which was silently received. She went on. 'It might mean nothing, but there was blood on the under sheet the other morning. I mean if it had been lower down I might have understood, but pillow cases suggest something kinky, but for the life of me I can't think what.'

I shrugged. 'Could have been a nose-bleed.'

'Maybe. But two towels were very badly stained and it wasn't all blood. Could have been pus or some kind of acid. And when I asked that sour-faced bitch of a maid if Madame required a doctor, she turned on me like a mad dog. Told me to mind my own business – not to talk about Madame. And later – well – she slipped as much as you've given me into my apron pocket.'

Anxiety took on several nasty shapes and not least among them was the shroud-draped figure of disease. And these days no one in my line can be certain he won't meet a virus that the medicos haven't cottoned onto yet. We'll leave that subject alone if you don't mind, not that it will bother me from now on.

Having left the chambermaid I went down to the kitchen and there renewed my acquaintanceship with old George who's been on the hotel cleaning staff long before I was born. He had developed a nose for smelling out the guest's private lives that would turn many a head snow-white if it were generally known.

He greeted me with a broad smile and pocketed my bank note with a fine air of unconcern.

'I see you've made it with the party in the Imperial Suite. And good luck to you I say. Do 'er for what you can and a bit more besides.'

I sank down on to a chair and accepted a cup of tea from a kitchen maid. 'Got anything on her, George?'

He sipped from a pewter mug before replying.

'Party – Princess Helena Landi – is well loaded, cleans 'er teeth twice a day, takes a bath every morning but don't shampoo 'er hair. Keeps three cut-throat razors in a small carrying bag wrapped up in face towels. The maid washes 'em in the bath every night. The towels, I mean.'

I scratched my head. 'Cut throat razors! What does she want them for? I mean if she needs shaving surely an electric razor would be the thing.'

'She's got one of those,' George hastened to add. 'Black hairs is washed down the lavatory pan.'

Having fished for and obtained all the information I could from the staff, I left the hotel and paid a visit to my tailor where

I made an appointment to be measured for a complete new wardrobe. I then went to my shoemakers.

I knew this must be one of my best assignments ever, but I experienced a strange reluctance to return to the hotel, resulting in my taking a long walk, a form of exercise foreign to my nature. But eventually the golden promise of more money drew me back.

*

I thoroughly enjoyed dining with the princess that evening, for she was a brilliant conversationalist and was clearly well-read, although I noticed a reluctance to give any details about her life. When I questioned her on this subject, a frown marred the smooth white brow and there came a gleam to her eyes, so I quickly began to talk of my life which soon restored her good humour. Information always comes to him who waits.

She wore a plain black dress that completely covered her from neck to ankles and this contrasted nicely with the treble row pearl necklace and the silver bangles that encircled each wrist. Her face was skilfully made up so that in the dim light she looked a well-preserved thirty-five.

The auburn wig had been exchanged for a blonde one and I again experienced a feeling of annoyance that this woman of the world who clearly had dress sense, had to spoil the general effect by wearing such a thick heavy monstrosity. Masses of silver blonde curls that reminded me of Bette Davis in *Whatever Happened to Baby Jane?* It made her appear top heavy and I couldn't dismiss the ridiculous notion that if she were to nod too abruptly it would land on the table with a resounding thud.

For starters she had two double malt whiskies and there wasn't a great deal left in the second bottle of strong Tuscan wine when she came to consider the possibility of a Cointreau with her coffee. Me, I made one glass of wine last a long time, for in my line of business a clear head is an absolute must. But I must admit she carried her liquor well for apart from a more apparent gleam in her eyes, I could not detect any change in her demeanour.

But she seemed to know a disconcerting lot about me. At one time my ire was raised by her mocking tone.

'What a pity, Chu-Chu, you haven't concentrated more time

to your other talent. I speak of book writing. I acquired two of your books from the public library and was impressed. Amazing for someone who left school at fourteen and worked as an errand boy in a butcher's shop. You have an unexpected sense of humour and an even more unexpected contempt for women. I wonder why that is? Then I detected a highly developed intelligence which is not all that surprising when one considers that your – how shall I put it? – caviare and champagne profession needs an exceptionally well-developed imagination. And is not imagination the dashing offspring of intelligence?'

I murmured: 'You flatter me, Madame.'

She waved a hand and I felt a need to grab it. 'Nonsense. I never flatter. I but report what I see or sense and it is surely nothing to your own merit if nature has given you a pleasant face and a fully active brain. You could just as easily have been born ugly and stupid. Again, despite the world's scorn, it would not have been your fault and merit only pity.'

'The rich,' I said, 'are always favoured. The formula for perfect happiness is health, wealth and the experience to enjoy both.'

I couldn't be certain if her smile was derisive or otherwise.

'You have wisdom! You have the power to fish truth from a very deep well! How splendid! Your entertainment value has been greatly enhanced. Now we can have what you English call jolly chats. The dark gods have decreed that we meet.'

I decided that the woman was more than eccentric – she must be at least slightly mad. The alcohol was having an effect, but not in the usual way. Instead of dulling, it was sharpening her senses. Those over-brilliant eyes locked their gaze with mine and something akin to a lazer beam swept across my brain. After a while, a smile came into being that reflected both sensuality and amusement.

My self-respect has been maintained by skilful double-thinking and concentrated will-power, while I have never lost sight of the fact that any kind of prostitution is based on hatred of the opposite sex. The kind of women who had need of my services were fundamentally masochists who revelled in the joys of anguish when indulging in the ultimate humiliation of having to pay for a young man's favours. But here I sensed a subtle difference: the princess barely masked a growing regard for me, a young man who sold his favours for hard cash or the brief ownership of a gold cigarette case. Her voice broke into my thought line.

'How old are you, Chu-Chu?'

I made an effort to bolster sagging self-respect. 'I would be grateful if you would not call me by that silly name.'

Her smile broadened. 'But it pleases me to call you Chu-Chu. As I said before – you look Chu-Chu. And it is my pleasure that must be considered, is that not so? I am the customer.'

I inclined my head. 'That is true but consideration for my feelings will make me happy.'

She began to wave her hands wildly as though waving off a flight of insects. 'Your feelings! If you suffer from delicate feelings then you have no place in my service. I have no feelings that need concern you. So long as you make me forget what I am for a few minutes, you may swear, insult – swear, I say – do what you bloody please. . .'

To my alarm she started to cry, sobbing loudly so that we became the focus for attention; waiters drifted within touching distance, quite prepared to intervene if anyone looked like threatening the tranquillity of their realm.

But the princess quickly regained control, veiled her eyes with half lowered lids, dismissed the frown, erased the grimace that bared teeth, then reaching out laid a cool hand over mine.

'Did I frighten the poor boy? To lose control of one's feelings is – how would you so correct English put it? – distasteful. Always keep stiff lips, the chin up, the shoulders erect.'

I spoke without due thought. 'Your English is not so correct.'

She nodded very slowly. 'So, you take note. I have allowed the curtains to part and thus permitted a glimpse of the *me* who came into being – long before your miserable little ego floated in on the sea of life. And eventually you will wish to take advantage of this growing familiarity – and I speak not of the pleasure we will share in bed – and it may well be I will be forced to take punitive action. Then would I weep. Not for you. For myself.'

We continued our meal and I deliberately did not speak,

until she at last chose to break the silence and began to mock me gently so I was made to feel like a sulky schoolboy.

'Have I again hurt the poor boy's feelings? Has the nasty old mama been thoughtless and talked as her tongue guided her? Are you giving her the silence punishment? Denying her the sound of your golden voice? Which is no more than she deserves. So I too will suffer in silence. Eat, drink, bottle my words. That is a good phrase, is it not? Bottle my words. One that you may use if it will profit you. Ah! Do I see the glimmer of a smile?'

'I am twenty-eight years of age, Madame.'

She raised both eyebrows and expelled her breath as a vast sigh.

'So! The answer to my question and a suggestion that you are not – despite your appearance and behaviour – a boy. Twenty-eight! A vast desert of time in which there must have been poured a deluge of experience. I must bow my head to a king of wisdom.'

'Indeed not, Madame. You so out-number me in years there can be no way I can match you in experience.'

She laughed softly but her eyes glowed like those of a suddenly aroused tigress. But her voice caressed even while it continued to mock.

'Once long, long ago, when *even* I was young and I still looked upon the world as a beautiful place, I owned an unusual pet. A coral snake. A very pretty creature with black and red bands. It used to coil round my wrist and push its little head up my sleeve. At times, such was my whim, I allowed it to sleep in my bosom, derived certain pleasure from its movement, even a kind of sensual excitement generated by the danger I courted. But my pretty little snake – now I believe it to have been very young – drank goat's milk and swallowed tiny field mice which I trapped for him and we were all in all to each other.

'Then one day I inadvertently trod on it and in an instant it drove sharp fangs into my ankle. Later I can show you the scar I bear. Poison raced through my bloodstream and I was ill for some time. My father, who did not know what he had sired, killed the snake which pained me more than the poison, for I still loved it dearly and I knew it would not have bitten me if I had not trodden upon it. But,' she looked at me, her eyes glittering like chips of coal in firelight, 'even today I know the danger of clasping a snake to my bosom, no matter what devotion it pretends.'

I captured her hand and raised it to my lips. 'Such a snake, Helena, that has the honour of entry to your bosom while it plots treachery deserves to be ground under a very heavy foot.'

'Your allegory fits very neatly on to the end of my parable,' she said softly, 'and it is possible we now understand one another a little better than five minutes ago.'

She did not speak again until the coffee cups had been removed, then she rose and without looking at me said quietly:

'I am going to bed but there is no need for you to do so unless you wish. But I will be pleased if you would be in your room not later than one o'clock. If I require your presence I will ring a bell that is situated over your bed. I had it installed today. If I have not rung by one-thirty I shall not do so tonight. Is that clear?'

'You are the soul of clarity.'

'Very well.' She extended a hand which I kissed. 'There is no need for you to accompany me back to our suite. The evening is young, so are you, so enjoy yourself. But do not seek the company of another woman. For the time being you are my property. Please to understand that.'

'I am yours until death and beyond.'

'This is not the time for pretty speeches neither do I welcome them. At the moment and for most of the evening you have behaved like a silly schoolboy and I must confess to being a little disappointed.'

And having delivered this stinging remark she left me and I – who have always maintained that you can form a much clearer view of character from the back of the head than the face – decided that the lady could never be anything but a tigress pretending to be a pussy cat.

I wandered around, completely at a loss as to know what to do with myself. There was plenty of business on the hoof and had my services not been engaged I could have made several worthwhile contacts. There was one woman in particular who attracted my attention. A medium-sized white-faced creature with large really lovely eyes. I assumed she was around thirty and well-heeled for the black velvet dress and diamond necklace hadn't been picked up in a church jumble sale and she looked the type that would suffer wonderfully in mink.

And those lovely dark eyes watched me with a flattering – if rather disconcerting – intensity. Also I soon had reason to believe she was following me around. Or perhaps it would be more accurate to say she preceded me wherever I went.

In the bar she was perched on a tall stool watching my reflection in the massive mirror behind the bar. I had been ordered not to form a contact with another woman, but I would not have been human to ignore this unsolicited attention, so I smiled and inclined my head.

Instantly she recoiled, shrank back as though I were a snake that had threatened to strike, and her eyes glittered in the most eerie way, I sensed anger, even hatred. Then I bumped into someone which distracted my attention and when I next turned my head she was gone.

She next materialized in the crowded foyer, seated on one of those green leather club chairs, still observing me with an unblinking stare. By now I was seriously alarmed. In my not unsuccessful career I have made many enemies – most of them women – and, believe me, if you're in the market for a sound, no-nonsense hater, look no further than the nearest scorned woman. I have trained my brain never to forget the face of a client or anyone who is closely connected with her – such as Gredelsa and the princess – but the mystery woman rang no bells, so I decided to approach her and if necessary twist her arm until I was told what this continuous staring was all about.

But getting close to her proved to be an insurmountable problem. As I have said, the foyer was crowded and when I pushed my way towards the chair on which the woman was seated, it was only to discover I must have been mistaken as to the location, for she was still staring at me from another chair some distance away. Having changed direction I lost her completely until I spotted her standing by the reception desk.

Gentlemen, I was reared on a diet of commonsense which stressed that that which can be seen, felt, smelt and listened to, exists, whereas that which is sensed, is connected in some way with second sight, intuition, table-rapping and such like, does not exist. Belongs to the realm of crackpotism.

On the other hand when one has exhausted the obvious,

worn out the possible, explored every avenue of conjecture, then must one seriously consider facing up to the improbable.

A dark-eyed woman wearing a black velvet dress who could transport herself from one place to another in a matter of seconds had to be considered under the heading – Improbable.

Rage and fear drove me through the crowd ignoring curses, shouted ironic enquiries and one quite hard punch, only to find the lady had taken up a new position by the lift.

I eventually gave up and went to my room, but when I walked to the window and looked down into the brilliantly lit street, she was standing in a shop doorway on the opposite side of the street, looking up.

I closed the curtains and prepared – in one way or another – for a sleepless   night.

CHAPTER TWO

I took a shower, put on a new pair of satin pyjamas and a green dressing gown, then lay down on the bed. The bedside clock pointed its hands to fifteen minutes to one when the overhead bell rang. A hideous clanging that should have awakened every sleeper in the hotel.

I stood up, went over to the dressing table and combed my hair. I looked right. Healthy, wealthy and beautiful. My assets would have been wasted in any other profession, with the possible exception of the film industry. I also, despite the episode of the strange dark woman, felt on top form. The master with magic in his fingers. The expert who could play a full symphony on a woman's body which was guaranteed to give her five orgasms in as many seconds. Boasting, gentlemen? No, advertising.

My quilted slippers made no sound when I moved out into the hall, then walked swiftly towards the door which I knew led to the princess's bedroom. My hand was raised to turn the handle when the door suddenly opened and Gredelsa was pushing me back, both hands pressed against my chest while she shouted at me with decidedly ragged English.

'Not not come in . . . pretty boy not come in . . . Madame changed her mind. Out . . . out . . . you puffee. . .'

I had a glimpse of the soles of the princess's feet which were dangling over the bottom of the divan and it was clear she was lying on her stomach covered by a pink sheet. An enamel kidney-shaped dish and an open cut-throat razor lay on the floor. But I had yet to allow a servant to dictate to me and I raised my voice and shouted:

'Is this true, Madame? You do not wish to see me?'

I was moments away from having my face clawed by Gredelsa when I, who had no compunction about hitting a woman, rammed a clenched fist under her ill-shaped nose, while the other pressed into her stomach. My left foot pushed down hard on the toes of her right and she released a gasp. I called out again:

'Will you assure me, Madame, you do not require my help and do not wish to see me?'

There was a long silence during which Gredelsa and I glared at each other, then the princess's voice came from the bed. It sounded hoarse, tremulous, but perfectly clear.

'Yes, I wish to see you. Just allow Gredelsa to – put me right – tidy up the room. . .'

Gredelsa emitted what I can only describe as a snarl as she slowly withdrew into the bedroom, slamming the door in my face. I returned to my own room and while waiting for the bell to ring again looked out of the window. The strange woman had disappeared.

When some half an hour had passed without the bell ringing I went out into the hall and pressed my left ear against the princess's bedroom door and was rewarded, if that is the right word, by hearing a heated argument between the two women, conducted again in the language I did not understand, although I did hear the silly non-de-plume with which I had been saddled, uttered by the princess.

Then the bell rang in my bedroom and after waiting for a few minutes, I tapped on the door and without waiting for an invitation, turned the handle and entered the room.

My client was wearing an old-fashioned white nightgown decorated with embossed pink flowers that was not all that becoming. Neither was the quilted cap that covered her head, neck and so far as I could see buttoned under her chin. It looked not unlike a monstrous tea cosy, even though by framing her face it did give her an innocent quality, very similar to that suggested by a nun's wimple. She was lying on the top of the bed, the pink sheet screwed up into the rough semblance of a rope, but the enamel kidney-shaped dish and cut-throat razor had disappeared. She gave me a brilliant smile and held out her right hand for me to kiss, and when she spoke for the first time her voice was really gentle, even kindly and she radiated an unexpected charm that had the effect of putting me at my ease. Her genial manner was even extended to the glowering Gredelsa.

'Gredelsa, you may leave us now. Try to get some rest, then you won't be so overwrought.'

Gredelsa shrugged extravagantly and raised her eyes ceilingward.

'Overwrought, she says! Madame, you know what's to be done and, if you're not careful, so will this young mortal. In fact I think he should be told.'

The princess spat. I mean just that. She spat a gob of saliva on to the bedside rug, then wiped her lips on the back of her hand. I hoped she wouldn't expect me to kiss it in the near future. She also spat out words.

'You want to break his sanity? He will know soon enough, but by then he'll be well prepared. He is of the right type, I tell you.'

'How can you be sure?'

'My mind tells me. Now go.'

Gredelsa stumped from the room after giving me a glance that was part contempt, part pity. The princess patted the bed and smiled gently. 'Come and sit by me, Chu-Chu. Let us get to know each other. Lovers should first be friends, is that not so?'

I nodded while wondering in what weird set-up I would be expected to play a role.

'Lay back against the headboard,' the princess ordered. 'Relax and just listen. Never mind if your environment will not allow you to believe all that I tell you. Just say to yourself the crazy woman is playing with imagination toys, but she is paying me and the customer must be humoured. Can you do that, Chu-Chu?'

I nodded, realising I was stuck with the silly nickname and there was no way I could get her to discard it.

'Say yes,' she ordered. 'Merely nodding is very rude.'

'Yes, Madame.'

'That's better. Let me start from the very beginning. I was born a very long time ago.'

The computer in my brain automatically sent out two words.

'Surely not!'

'Please, do not play the role of enslaved lover now. This is a time for serious talk. Let me begin again. I was born a very, very long time ago. If I told you just how long you would smile that patient disbelieving smile that Englishmen know how to assume so easily. My father was a prince in the land of Cashma – it is known by a far different name now – and I, out of the fifty or so children he had sired, was his favourite. He raised me as a boy would have been reared and educated and I could out ride, fight and think any man in his army – including Abul his personal bodyguard.

'I can remember the night long rides, the dawn attack, the drug-like ecstasy that can only be experienced in the heat of battle. Then the ride home accompanied by the sobbing cries of the captives, the moans of the wounded and the roar of the wind which we interpreted as Allah's approval.'

All this sounded like a weak plot from a novelette with *The Sheik's Daughter* pretensions. But she was relating it as someone who is reaching back through long avenues of time, where the light of memory still burned brightly. Indeed it would seem she intended me to believe these events occurred in some far distant period, but I could not believe she was more than fifty, even considerably younger. I think she could read my thoughts for she patted my hand and said:

'You must learn to have faith in Helena. I tell you nothing less than the truth and indeed why should I lie when the patterns that make up my life are more fantastic than any fictional plot dreamed up by a professional creator of fantasies – such as yourself, Chu-Chu.'

After a while I leaned over and kissed her on the lips, a long, lingering caress with my mouth barely touching hers. When she would have put a hand behind my head, I pulled back and tantalized her by flickering tongue and murmured words of protest.

'No, Helena, that is not the way. You must walk the road of a thousand deaths, then endure a world-shattering rebirth, then die again . . . again. . .'

At first I thought she was aroused, but after a while she shook her head making the padded cap quiver in the strangest way, then said quietly:

'Chu-Chu, I am certain many of your clients fully appreciate your technique and profit by it, but you will find I am strangely – yes, I use that word without hesitation – strangely constituted. I want you to listen to me very carefully. Stroke my head very gently, but do not press – not yet – or poke with your fingers. Above all, never attempt to touch or move my head cover. Is that quite clear?'

I successfully acquired a pained expression.

'Never would I –'

Hers took on a menacing quality. 'And never will you repeat, not even to yourself in the privacy of your room, what takes place here. Do so – and I will be forced to take steps you will not like. Not like at all.'

I deepened my pained expression.

'I was about to state that never would I violate the intimacy of the bedroom and I am very hurt that you should even consider such a possibility. I am, Madame, both a professional and a gentleman.'

Her eyes closed, her voice became a purr.

'Never mind being a pro-gentleman, just do as I order. Stroke my head – and be very careful.'

There was a reluctance to raise my hands and touch that quilted cover and run fingers down it, then across, while Madame issued her instructions, the urgency in her voice making me nervous and wonder what to hell I'd let myself in for.

'Careful . . . careful . . . that's it . . . you're poking too deeply . . . don't move the cap . . . don't move it. . .'

I spoke thoughtlessly, but reasonably: 'I can't imagine why you wear it. It must be very hot.'

She snatched her head away and glared up at me while her head shook in the most alarming fashion. 'Have I not made myself clear? Repeated myself until my voice grows hoarse from exhaustion? The head cover must not, *must not* be disturbed, not even if the world is coming to an end. Little puffee, are you stupid or deaf? Or both?'

I began a silent but very eloquent protest at these insults and was at once rebuked by a voice that was barely below a scream.

'And do not sulk. You are paid to do what I tell you and suffer such chastisement as pleases me.'

'Look here. . .'

'And do not interrupt. You will in the fullness of time see my naked head and when that time comes I will take joy from your cries of admiration.' Suddenly she reached out and patted my hands. 'Try to understand. An over-abundance of knowledge, revelation can be dangerous. The sanity is fragile – I know of what I speak – and is apt to break if over-burdened. Possess your soul in patience and just lightly caress my head. Then you will again become my sweet Chu-Chu whom I will love most dearly and give him two – no – three hundred pounds over and above his salary. Now, do you not feel much better?'

I did. For me, money was the panache that would negate the ill-effects of insults, enrich both body and soul, turn a scowl into a beaming smile. The kind of smile I have perfected and only reveal on special occasions. This was one such occasion.

'Allow me to continue your massage, Princess. My fingers will ease the tension. The brain will shimmer so delightfully and then we will –'

'Just do what I told you to do and not so much talk.'

I got the hang of it after a while. It was rather like trying to tap out a muted tattoo on a kettle drum. The padding was thick, but not so thick I could not detect certain protuberances rather like boils, and every now and again an impression of stealthy movement, a kind of writhing, although at that time I decided this was imagination aided possibly by a shifting of kapoc padding. After some minutes the princess murmured:

'Just a little harder, Chu-Chu. I cannot forego you pressing just a little harder. But be careful. You have such wonderful hands. A delightful touch. No one before . . . ah!'

All this was all very well although I was beginning to wonder when we would get down to serious business, when my fingers detected distinct movement. There could be no doubt, a side to side and up and down movement, followed by a dampness, moisture. I thought: boils. Her head is covered by boils and I'm making them burst. What the hell is it like under that padded thing?

But the princess was in ecstasy; little moaning sounds were coming from her partly open mouth and there were movements all over her head, causing me to shrink back in disgust and I would have run from that room, only a hand with an iron grip pulled me towards her. Her eyes were glazed and slightly crossed and I was aware of a slightly acid smell that is sometimes given off by certain animals when either excited or frightened.

Her voice was low and husky. 'You must learn to accept. I

am not a monster, not a real monster. Please to sit still and . . . and . . . if it is not too much for you to bear, dig your fingers deep. Stay with me and do all I ask and I will make you a rich man. You'd like that . . . dig deeper . . . dig deeper. . .'

The lure of gold was irresistible, so I again raised my hands to that moist head-cover and did as she asked – but I closed my eyes when thick clear fluid seeped down over her forehead and even more down the back of her neck; but I managed to keep the massage going, dug my fingers into writhing something, then the movement and the smell became more than I could bear and with a muffled cry I finally fled. Raced out into the hall where Gredelsa was waiting and she, after one swift glance at my face, ran into the bedroom and slammed the door.

I started to pack my bags but soon realised that I would need many more to hold all the new clothes I had bought at the princess's expense – and this fact made me pause. She had promised to make me a rich man which could mean I was about to run away from a fortune. But what the hell was the matter with her?

Hidden by day under a large wig and a great padded bag at night was a mass of ripening boils. And those ripening boils burst when caressed, kneaded – rubbed.

But my clientele were not noted for their beauty or state of well-being and I had always coped before, once I had been convinced that there wasn't anything catching.

Number one question: were the princess's boils catching?

I decided to suspend packing until after I had held an all important interview with Gredelsa.

Twice she passed me in the hall but was far too occupied to pay heed to me, carrying on one occasion an enamel bowl that was half filled with blood-stained water. This was deposited into the lavatory pan which Gredelsa flushed three times. Then the bedroom door was slammed again and I was able to hear another argument going on, uttered unfortunately in that foreign tongue, although I did decide that Gredelsa was advising a course of action with which the princess did not agree.

There followed two more visits to the bathroom where the lavatory pan was again flushed three times and the maid seemed to be on the verge of collapse. I considered this to be extraordinary as she had always struck me as being a creature with an unlimited reserve of strength, but when she staggered and sank to the floor, I swooped like a bird of prey and carried the senseless body into my own room where I flung it on the bed. After half a tumbler of whisky had been poured down her throat Gredelsa moaned, then opened her eyes and stared up at me with wide-eyed alarm. She ejected strangled words:

'What for are you . . . you . . . in my room?'

'You are in my room,' I corrected gently. 'You fainted in the hall and I brought you in here.'

The fear faded from her eyes and was replaced by a cautious gleam. She half rose up on her elbows, then with a muffled gasp fell back again. She now regarded me with a speculative air. She spoke slowly.

'Unlike the others you did not run away or be sick over the carpet. Maybe you have more than a pretty face.'

'What's wrong with her?' I asked.

She shook her head. 'That is for Madame to say if she wishes you to know.'

'But you will admit she has some kind of disease?'

Another violent shaking of the head. 'I will admit nothing. Maybe she is suffering from boils. Nasty boils that burst and old Gredelsa has to bathe.'

'Are they catching?' I asked.

'Catching?'

'Infectious?'

She may have spoken impulsively, her normal defence mechanism made faulty by stress, for she said: 'Only if you're bitten.'

The words had been spoken and could never be recalled and their effect on my sub-conscious will never be erased. My mind leapt from one high point to another. Conjecture consumed conjecture and brought forth horrific possibility.

Lice! A swarm of disease carrying vermin. Or maybe the lady when overcome by sexual passion bit – and ejected venom into her partner's bloodstream. Surely horrific impossibility.

'Bitten!' I repeated. 'Bitten by what?'

'Nothing that need concern you. You have had money. I will try to get you more. Leave now. Others have gone mad when they learn the truth. There is much you will never understand

. . . much that takes place in a country beyond this. . . I can speak no more.'

I leaned over her, placed a hand on either side of the bed so that she was confined by my arms, and looked down into her eyes. I saw the flickering fires of fear that I had ignited in her brain.

'I can never solve riddles,' I confessed. 'So stop hinting. What is likely to bite me?'

'Nothing. Just a term of speech. You forget English is not my native tongue. I can tell you nothing. Only Madame can do that. Why concern yourself. You only here for money.'

I bent over until I could see my face reflected in her eyes; the beads of sweat erupting on her forehead.

'Again, until the cows come home, what is likely to bite me?'

'Nothing. Maybe Madame herself.'

'Is her bite lethal?'

'Not lethal. Madame not bite, nothing bite.'

'What is really wrong? What causes the boils? Why do you have to lance them? Why not call in a doctor? There is one contracted to this hotel. I can have him here within ten minutes.'

Now she really lost control, screamed at me in broken English, sometimes lapsed into the foreign tongue, even while she tried to break free from my retaining grip.

'You are a fool, stupid fool who know nothing about anything soon will die with popped out eyes . . . die . . . or go mad. . .'

My hands gripped her shoulders and shook her until she could not speak, then I again repeated the by now familiar question.

'What is likely to bite me? What can give me an infectious bite?'

When I ceased shaking her she remained still for some little while, then the fear faded from her eyes to be replaced by a gleam of pure malice, or anger that burned with a cold flame.

She said slowly: 'So pretty boy want to know the truth! Madame the Princess will be very angry when she know I told you, but that does not matter, I have endured her anger before. Lower your so beautiful head so I can whisper the truth you so much want to hear, then I will see the love light burn brightly in your eyes. Hear your cries of joy.'

I did indeed lower my head and waited for the harsh whisper to utter the truth I did not really want to hear. It exploded in my brain.

'You could be bitten by a snake.'

I asked another question. 'You mean she keeps a venomous snake in her bedroom? In her bed?'

How the hag cackled, laughed with unholy joy before spitting out words I would never forget.

'Not keep, pretty boy, but grow. Madame the Princess does not just keep snakes – she grows them. On her head and if one bites you, you too will grow snakes . . . somewhere.'

Now it was my turn to try to break free but her hands gripped my arms and I was pulled gasping from pure terror down towards her black-toothed mouth.

'Bitten once – one snake – bitten twice – three snakes. I bitten once. Would you like to see my little friend? I . . . I . . . cut him off like I do for princess, but grow again thicker. Tiny at first and pretty, then bigger, peep out over dress top. Those on belly go for navel, those in thigh go for . . . ha, ha . . . ha.'

Then I found the strength to break free before dragging her from the bed. I shouted horror-fear rage and pointed to the door. 'Get out, you poor mad cow. You're sick . . . sick. . .'

She looked back at me from the doorway.

'Listen to me, pretty boy, take what money she give you, then go. Don't play games anymore. Soon we go to Far Acres and once there you lost. Perish in the Red River, be swallowed by the ele-snake. I not hate you. Just pity, and fear. Ah! Fear.'

With that she closed the door leaving me to lie on the bed and think strange thoughts all night.

During the night I believed and suffered many cold shivers for my belief. Come morning, I began to have doubts. When the sun was well up over the roof tops I laughed at myself for being such a credulous fool.

The real truth was so apparent.

Gredelsa was jealous and not a little worried and she had chosen an unique way to scare me off. I was willing to believe the princess suffered from some sort of complaint which resulted in fearsome boils on her head, this being the reason she kept it well covered by wig and padded nightcap. But even to imagine she grew snakes, and venomous ones to boot, was the height of fantastic thinking. In the golden light of a summer day it seemed impossible that I had not treated Gredelsa's account as the raving of a mad woman.

I took a shower, enjoyed a light breakfast, then went out for a shave and a manicure; then, feeling more like my old self, I went to pay my respects to the princess.

Having knocked on the door and being told to enter, I found my lady sitting up in bed wearing a pink bed-jacket and a matching head-cover – and looking more disturbing than the night before.

Her face was deeply lined, chalk-white, the pouched eyes gleamed bright as though with excitement or fever; and all my so recently dismissed fear flared up again with renewed life.

Yet I could sense rather than see the faint ghost of an erstwhile breathtaking beauty – and there came to me the first stirring of pity, and emotion that up to that time I had little experienced, and it was this that caused me most disquiet, for if a man cannot trust his inner self, allows sentiment, anger, love or pity to snatch control of his brain, then he is on the road to complete destruction.

My knees did not knock when I approached the bed, but they should have; my hands did not tremble when they gripped hers, but only the dark gods know where I found the self-control which kept them steady.

I asked: 'You have recovered from – your attack?'

She slid her hands over my wrists, her fingers causing a not unpleasant tickling sensation to run up my arms. I was then given a doting smile.

'I feel much better thank you, Chu-Chu. The pressure is much less than last night. And you? You have recovered from the disposition that caused you to flee from my bedroom?'

'I have indeed and must ask your forgiveness for that moment of weakness.'

She gripped my hands even tighter and I could swear there was the suspicion of tears in her eyes.

'There is nothing to forgive, dear Chu-Chu. The fact you can re-enter my bedroom with a bright smile and an enquiry as to my well-being, is a matter for my gratitude. In fact it has made me feel so well I have decided to go for a long walk. That will be good for me, will it not?'

I smilingly nodded. 'That will be very nice, but you must not overdo it.'

She emitted a throatly chuckle. 'What a kind Chu-Chu you are. And that so English expression: don't overdo it. That covers so many activities, does it not? But now you must leave me to Gredelsa who will make me worthy of being seen walking beside such a handsome young man.'

I kissed her hand – having no option of doing otherwise – exchanged glares with Gredelsa who at that moment entered the room, then went out and lay down on my own bed, there to try and separate fact from conjecture, remember what I had been told, seen and did not believe. At least that was my intention.

Lying on a comfortable bed plus serious thinking has the effect of wooing sleep and in no time at all I was floating over a purple field where white-eyed reptiles stared up at a fire-tinted, cloud-racked sky.

It had always been a cause of amazement to me that my dreams were so vivid I could recall every incident with the utmost clarity. Also in that strange land I had the ability to fly without any effort and could moreover transfer from one place to another by merely thinking myself there. But this was the first time I had visited the reptile land.

On this occasion I looked down – in my dream – and saw the princess walking slowly through a grey ground mist, stepping over reptilian bodies seemingly unafraid of their gaping jaws, and I could see – with rising excitement – that she was now young and beautiful and her head was covered with a glorious cascade of red-gold hair that hung down to her shoulders. She wore a flimsy gown studded with diamonds or some other glittering gems and her beautiful eyes seemed to reflect an inner light, and a voice somewhere close to hand whispered: 'This is an immortal being who amuses herself by walking the floor of hell.'

And I began to descend, drawn by the magic of those eyes, even though hideous heads stirred as though with anticipation and a foul wind sprang up and with it came an ever-increasing whispering voice that presently roared: 'Netjer-Ankh . . .

Netjer-Ankh. . .' And her beauty glowed in the suddenly pulsating red light and, thanks be to those who watched over me, just as I was about to enter the haunted mist that swirled about her slim form, an ear-splitting clamour of the electric bell dragged me back into spluttering, sweat-drenched wakefulness, sobbing for – I knew not what.

*

A hired car took the princess and me out into the countryside and we lunched at one of those tarted-up wooden beam and horse brasses, so-called country pubs, where it cost a tenner to sit down and another to open the giant menu.

'I am famished,' Helena informed me, 'and am willing to eat a horse if it has been slowly cooked in red wine and garnished with parsley sauce. But, Chu-Chu, have you ensured that our driver has what he needs? A full lunch less intoxicating liquid, on the understanding he does not occupy a table in this dining room.'

'All taken care of,' I replied, knowing the chauffeur would have pocketed the twenty pounds I gave him and was now enjoying a ham sandwich and a glass of beer in the pub lower down the road.

My lady as usual ate well and I, still under the influence of that vivid dream, found myself studying her even while I maintained a bright flow of conversation.

Today she wore an over-large black wig and in the full light of day looked haggard and old, there being little resemblance to that glorious creature I had seen looking up at me in the dream land. There remained a faint ghost of that god-like beauty, but to summon it from the grave of long dead years, one must replace that awful wig with a glorious cascade of red-gold hair, rebuild the face, using the fine bone structure as a foundation, the body – well – it might not require all that reconstruction, a little padding maybe. And she – at times radiated undimmed youth, at others impossible age.

Her voice, now young, tinged with amusement, broke my line of thought.

'Chu-Chu, you are miles away and have not heard a word I have said. Fie on you.'

Instantly I became the epitome of solicitous attention,

denying – with false tongue – that I had missed a single word of what she had been saying and telling her I approved of everything that pleased her and disapproved of every action that might displease her. Thereupon she laughed most heartily and vowed I had the wittiest tongue of anyone she had ever known and she was more than pleased with me and would consider buying me a rich gift the very next morning.

It was then I spotted the dark woman who had so worried me the night before; she was standing against the wall to the right of the bar watching the princess with hatred blazing from her dark eyes; and she now wore an amber-coloured dress. She emitted – or so I thought – a blend of loneliness, misery and hatred.

Happiness, joy and the very essence of life were instantly blighted and a shudder quivered across my brain. Madame gave me one swift glance, then snapped:

'What is it? What is wrong?'

Instinct warned me I should not tell her, but there was no way I could keep such information to myself.

'That woman, over there by the bar, I saw her last night. I think . . . I think she is dead.'

How slowly did Madame the Princess turn her head and how strange was it that her face which up to that moment I thought to be as pale as any living face could be, turned to the whiteness of freshly fallen snow. I knew both of their stares had locked even though my lady's head was turned and I could see the quiver of rage that ran down the entire length of her body and heard the loud harsh whisper that seemed to rasp across my brain.

'Am I to have no peace? I did not send the great snake to seek you out. When the curse is lifted from me, you will be free again. Offend me – offend Netjer-Ankh. But I had no hand in it.'

The woman in the bright amber dress glided rather than walked and at length stood looking down at the princess, her face now a mask of hate. Then Helena raised her right hand and spoke in a strange tongue that seemed compiled from hissing consonants – and instantly the woman shrank back and gave the impression she was writhing in her dress, before wringing her hands, turning and drifting back across the room. She vanished before reaching the door. The princess gazed upon me with glittering eyes and fired questions with the rapidity of a machine gun.

'Do you feel weak? Are you shivering? Strangely tired? Coldness in the stomach? Speak, man.'

After some thought I said: 'There is a cold feeling in my stomach and around my neck and shoulders. But weakness – no.'

She nodded. 'You are a strong young man in excellent health, but I would say you have been feeding Fiona. Allowing her to build up and take on a shape that looks considerably older than the one she had in earth life. You have much power, it drew me to you when we first met, but I never thought you would attract an outcast. But I have banished her to the underworld. Now –'

'You must finish your lunch,' I stressed, 'or you will never grow up to be a strong girl.'

She giggled, a not very appealing sight or sound, and looked at me with much affection, indeed causing me even more concern for an over-loving client can become a menace that refuses to be dismissed once the assignment is completed. But now she spoke nothing less than the truth.

'You are a most remarkable young man for I know of none other who has viewed for the first time a rebuilt unbodied and not expressed terror.'

I shrugged. 'I have learnt to accept whatever experience that comes my way and try to decide why and how. To give way to fear is the height of stupidity.'

To my great alarm tears appeared in her eyes and her left hand slid across the table and gripped mine. When she spoke her voice trembled. 'You are the one for whom I have searched all these centuries. You must never leave me. Accept what I am and try to find a solution, then will you be rewarded as no man since the beginning of time. But, Chu-Chu, disaster could so well overwhelm us both.'

My appetite died a swift death and I laid down my knife and fork and tried to ignore the plate of spaghetti bolognese that the princess began to attack with unusual gusto. She looked at my barely touched portion and coyly repeated my earlier instruction to her.

'You must finish your lunch or you'll not grow up to be a big strong boy.'

*

The princess summoned me to her bed that night.

Despite growing confidence that I could handle any situation that might arise, I entered her bedroom with some trepidation, not helped by Gredelsa's sneering grin. My lady wore a baby doll transparent nightie and another quilted night cap.

For the first time since I had known her she looked happy and there could be no doubt by the way she pawed me, I was the reason. She could barely wait for me to shed the dressing gown and climb into bed beside her before clawing at my pyjama jacket, ripping off three buttons and shredding the material with her sharp pointed nails. Her flickering tongue did a sound ear-washing job, her teeth ventilated my neck so that I shed blood in a most unworthy cause, while her left hand seemed to be trying to strangle my number one commercial asset. At one point I may have shrieked and fought her off, finally to take control by gripping both of her wrists and pressing them into the padded headboard.

This battle of battles raged for at least three hours, or maybe not so long, but when both of us sank into a sleep of sheer exhaustion it did seem as if we'd been at it for three years. The bedside lamps were left burning for the princess liked to see what she was doing, but they didn't bother me for I was in no condition to do more than shut my eyes and let my ego go spinning down into a red pit.

I came awake suddenly. Came up from that pit with the abruptness of a rocket leaving its pad, found I was covered with a sheen of perspiration and shaking like an old man who has just seen death limping down a long corridor towards him.

I did not move but lay with my head still embedded in a well-filled pillow, in a position to see the princess who lay with head facing me. It took me a good ten seconds to understand what I actually saw. Then my brain, having accepted the information presented by my eyes, came up with an irrevocable decision.

A thin flesh-coloured snake with a pink head had wriggled down from under the padded cap and now lay on the princess's forehead. The thickness of my little finger, wrinkled in places; I had to assume that part which still remained hidden under the quilted cap was rooted to my lady's head. The pink head (I am referring to the snake's) was covered with what looked like a delicate finger nail, from which two microscopic red eyes glittered like tiny illuminated rubies. A cotton-thin red tongue flicked out now and again, possibly, and I'm still not certain about this, sucking up the princess's perspiration as a form of refreshment.

As I watched with unreliable bowels another fleshy reptile slid from behind the left ear, waving its head from side to side, then having spotted the first arrival hissed and spat green foam. The quilted cap began to heave as more of the creatures became aroused and I have since come to the conclusion that they all shared a primitive intelligence – if that is the right word – and when one or more emerged into the light, this had a disturbing effect on the entire nest.

By now I was not only terrified, but nauseated. That these awful writhing, heaving things were part of the princess's body, had to be the peak of grotesque horror and I only retained my place in her bed because – and this I blush to state – I had grown aware of a growing curiosity.

This besetting sin, we are told, killed the cat, but I am willing to go further and say it also dragged man up from the primeval swamp and put him on the way to the stars, even if it damned him to become a creature laden down with unwanted knowledge.

I can never read or even think of that horrible little word 'why?' without joining it to another wretched little word 'how?'

So it was I found myself asking 'why?' Madame the Princess had a crop of nasty flesh-coloured snakes growing on her head, and 'how?' they had come into being – and 'how?' were they able to maintain a separate form of life from the main body.

My hastily assembled thoughts decided *they* could be related to the maggot family although *they* did not consume the host body, but were nourished by the blood stream, plus liquid refreshment provided by the body moisture.

May I be forgiven, but curiosity – mine at least – has an insatiable appetite and having been but inadequately fed by conjecture began to wonder what the crop would look like when the head cover was completely removed. The princess was fast asleep, for our almost super-human performance had exhausted her to a state of collapse, and all I needed to do was untie two ribbons under her chin – or so I thought – to uncover her scalp.

No sooner had the thought come into being than my hands were moving headwards, only to recoil when four little pink heads hissed while the thin bodies suddenly became erect, shot upright and jerked in the direction of my intruding hands. A fleck of green foam splashed on to the left little finger and I lost no time in wiping the vile stuff away for it stung like fury and if left unattended might well have burnt the finger.

But I soon found I could get a grip on the quilted material at the very top and this I did, then, after taking a deep breath, jerked forward and up, thus making it unnecessary to risk being bitten by untying the chin ribbons.

They all stood up and waved their heads.

Rooted in red, boil-like bulges, I could now see they had blue-vein skins and averaged some four inches in length, save for those at the back that were considerably longer and overlay the short stubby ones (that had been cut) that coated the skull base and in some places covered the neck (where Gredelsa had not be allowed to trim them). The entire hideous mop were threshing wildly, several heads fighting among themselves, others becoming entangled; and the hissing chorus woke Madame.

She sat up and looked at me with eyes in which the spark of fear was just being ignited; then she raised her hands and like any woman newly aroused began to run fingers through her disturbed locks. Several heads opened their mouths and sank minute fangs into the back of her hands, and she shook them while emitting a wail of anguish.

'You wicked, wicked boy! What have you done? I've a good mind to make you kiss my hands better. Really I think. . .'

But I could not take any more – not then – not even if she had offered me five million in the bank, and I raced from the room and barely reached the bathroom in time to be sick in the wash basin. Then just as I was getting over this inexcusable weakness and was in a position to think about money again, I saw something swimming in the lavatory pan.

I went down to the bar and got drunk. Really and truly stinko, something I had never done before in my entire life.

CHAPTER THREE

I awoke next morning with the great-grandfather of a hangover and a half resolve to buy some extra travelling bags, pack everything that could be packed, then depart for places far away and snake-free. That was before I saw the envelope propped up on top of the tallboy, which when opened revealed a cheque for five hundred pounds. I decided to remain just a little longer, but prepared to put on my running shoes the very moment the situation became more than I or my stomach could stand.

I had toyed with eggs and bacon, drunk two cups of black coffee and was blinking owlishly with bleary eyes when Gredelsa presented herself at my table. She appeared to be more affable than normally. She even accepted my invitation to sit down even if she did perch herself on the edge of the chair and give the impression she might make a bolt for the lift if I so much as moved. Presently she said:

'I am surprised. Never before have I known one who remained with Madame once he even half suspected the truth. I always afraid one will tell the world about Madame's . . . illness. That is why I try to get rid of them quickly, like I did you. But if you can stay without too much fear and keep mouth shut and help me with Madame, then I will be able to – how do you put it? – relax sometimes.'

I grimaced and signalled to a waiter to pour me another cup of coffee, having come to a rapid conclusion it was much too early for anything stronger. Curiosity was again blending with horror and I was moving in a strange limbo where it did not seem to matter what happened to me so long as I was permitted to discover an *explanation* as to why the princess was afflicted with snakes growing on her head.

I asked suddenly: 'Are you infected?'

Her nod was barely perceptible.

'Trimming Madame's growth becomes necessary from time to time you understand and she does not like it being done. Cutting them is very painful and a nip can pass unnoticed, otherwise I would have used antidote. . .'

I quickly interrupted. 'There is one?'

'Oh, yes. At Far Acres the princess's – well – country house, she has a laboratory. By taking the venom from the creatures themselves it has been possible to make a serum.'

I had to ask one more very important question, but she would not allow me to finish.

'How did she –?'

'That I must not tell you. Madame will if she so wishes.'

'When will we go to the country house? Far Acres?'

'Any time now. Madame has done the business for which she came to this city and she will now wish to return to the one place where she can be . . . herself. If you stay – adapt – pass the great test, you will learn much, be rewarded as few mortals have been down the ages. You understand? When I become excited my English is not so good.'

Suddenly she smiled at me in a way she had never done before.

'I am glad we have become friends. I have never made a friend before. Never.'

Then I remembered the night before, removing the head cover, the princess raising her hands to her head, then my flight from the room. I shook my head.

'She will not take me anywhere. Not after last night. I uncovered her head – she was bitten on the hands.'

Gredelsa cackled softly. 'She afraid you not be here this morning. So long as you stay all is forgiven. In fact she will not now have to tell you about head condition. And you have not run away. Not gone mad. You be well rewarded. Much happiness and power wait for you at Far Acres. You see.'

She left me in a ridiculously happy state for which I could think of no justification, but this euphoria drove me to the princess's bedroom (being careful to knock on the door and wait for an invitation to enter first) where she was sitting up in bed wearing a gold embroidered head-cap and a matching bed-jacket. She greeted me with a cry of joy and held out her arms to embrace me.

I believe my half-simulated pleasure was totally convincing, for now that I had come to accept the bizarre, I could now appreciate this strange woman was not without a certain charm. Even when I sat next to her on the bed and looked into the haggard, over made-up face and knew what lay under the grotesque head cover, I could not disperse the illusion she was a beautiful woman who loved me.

She stroked my cheek with her left hand. 'Naughty boy to remove cap and cause my hands to be bitten. Look.'

She held out her hands palms uppermost and there on the soft white flesh were four red marks. She made what could have been a charming grimace on a young and pretty woman and said coyly: 'If you were truly sorry you would kiss them better.'

It was a beautiful hand and I now had no difficulty in doing what she wanted, even while she whispered not particularly enthralling information.

'I took fluid that Gredelsa always has with her and now they should not spread. Not more than already are. Tell me, Chu-Chu, would you like to leave this city and go into the country? Special country. Enjoy tranquillity, the silence absolute. Exist in the imperceptible mist of unreality. At Far Acres dreams can come true. If you try hard enough.'

I shrugged and looked deep into her eyes. I could see the coloured shadows that swirled in their depths, but did not quite make contact with the soul-searing memories that lurked there.

I said: 'There are bad dreams. And they come true as well.'

She nodded and the quilted head cover wobbled dangerously.

'I am the nightmare that drifts over the frontier that separates the Mad-Lands from the commonplace. Pray to the gods that I too become soft-hued fantasy.'

'When do we move to the country?' I asked.

'This morning.'

*

A gleaming Rolls-Royce car, followed by a green van in which was packed all our luggage, took us out of London immediately after lunch, with me seated beside the princess on the commodious back seat, while Gredelsa sat beside the chauffeur, her head erect, looking neither to left nor right, not all that happy because I now occupied the place which normally would have been hers.

Gradually the teeming city gave way to the more subdued suburbs, that in turn thinned out into straggling lines of cottages and the occasional farm house, widely separated by cultivated fields and shadow-haunted woods.

The princess pressed a switch that was set in the arm of her part of the seat and spoke into a tiny microphone.

'Conrad.'

A man's deep voice seemed to come from the roof and it took me some time to realise it was that of the chauffeur.

'My lady?'

'Speed up and sideways.'

There was a slight pause before the deep voice spoke again.

'If you insist, my lady.'

I saw a frown crease her forehead. 'I do. Speed up and sideways.'

'The universal time, . . .'

'Do as I order.'

'Your word is my command, Madame the Princess.'

I tried to see what our driver looked like for up to then I had assumed he was employed by a car-hire firm, but it would now seem he was in the princess's service, and therefore someone I should cultivate. But all I could see was a fat white neck surmounted by thick black hair and a pair of grey eyes that watched me – or so I thought – from the rear mirror.

The even purr of the engine rose to a shrill whine and I was forced back on to the upholstery as the car gathered speed, but when I looked out of the window I all but passed out when I tried to come to terms with what I saw.

Normally when one looks from a speeding car window it seems as if hedgerows, houses and walls are racing backwards; but from the Rolls window I was being subjected to a completely different effect. Trees, fields – all – appeared to be racing to keep up with us, while further away I saw what had to be an old manor house suddenly disappear. I opened my mouth to ask some very pertinent questions, but the princess waved an impatient hand.

'Not now, Chu-Chu. All will be explained later. Suffice to say I am bored with this dimension and as I do not have to remain here I'm not going to do so. If what you see from the window upsets you, close your eyes.'

When I again looked out of the window I was tempted to do so for now the countryside was rushing away from us – sideways. A hawthorn hedge seemed to rise up from the ground then go racing backwards to the far horizon, only to be replaced by rolling moorland, which was followed by a range of hills, then acres of cultivated ground. When I looked out of the rear window I could see that although the road remained constant, the vista on both sides was rushing forward.

Gredelsa's voice came from the overhead speaker: 'Madame, the staff at number two level will not be expecting us.'

The princess jerked her head and never before had I seen her look so angry.

'Gredelsa, don't be so silly. You know the truth, no one – apart from myself – more so.'

'Yes, Madame, but one doesn't always wish to face truth.'

'We have no option.'

The chauffeur spoke: 'We are about to enter the time-mist, Madame.'

'Very well, then drive carefully. It would be a disaster if we were to go off the track.'

'Of that I am fully aware, Madame.'

Suddenly all light was blotted out and I could see black whirling mist that seemed to be trying to force its way through the windows which I now noticed were hermetically sealed, air being drawn into the car by means of extractor fans set in the roof.

Never before had I seen black mist, for there was no way it could be confused with smoke. In part it glistened as though reflecting some distant source of light, and when Helena turned on the interior lights I could see my own face in the window glass, then seemingly retreat into that awful black stuff, so that it looked like a disembodied head staring in with fear-bright eyes.

The chauffeur's voice came again from the loudspeaker.

'It will be necessary, Madame to turn on the headlights. The mist becomes even thicker later on. I thought it would be so at this universal time. But Madame the Princess would. . .'

The princess turned to me and laid a gentle hand on mine.

'Chu-Chu, it might be well if you closed your eyes now or allow me to blindfold you. The headlights will reveal much that can be very upsetting to anyone who has not been through the time mists before.'

I had no doubt she spoke nothing less than the entire truth, but my own particular curse – curiosity – told me if I closed my eyes, did not look upon whatever was revealed by the car headlights, I would spend the rest of my life wondering what it was I had not seen.

'Gredelsa always looks,' the princess murmured in my left ear.

That of course settled the question once and for all.

'My eyes will remain open,' I said.

'My foolish but brave Chu-Chu, but no more than I expected. For did not the prophet say: "In the Shadow Lands the jackal will take on the habiliments of the lion and turn fear into a spur." You must be the one who was promised.'

But I was in no condition to solve the riddles she set me, for at that moment the car headlights carved twin tunnels through the whirling black mist and I could see those that floated, danced, or simply stared at the car as it passed.

Gentlemen, I find difficulty in describing those creatures, the mere appearance of which threatened to shatter that state I was pleased to call my sanity.

I am sure – I sincerely hope – they had no substantial existence. They changed shape too often for that. On the other hand they could have been formed from some kind of plastic, existed in a way that cannot be explained in man's limited vocabulary.

The drifting skeleton with the bulbous head that seemed to be wrapped in an over-abundance of semi-transparent skin – that sometimes became a round faintly green ball that bounced against our car window which seemed to be a frail barrier between me and it. Then the tall thin white – something – that sent out long coils each one capped by a round face with bulging blue eyes, that had a haunting familiarity, rather like a childhood nightmare that is remembered in well advanced adulthood.

Then the small ones. How strange that my mind – as it is now – has started to banish their likeness from the realm of memory so that their outline is becoming blurred. But I must do my best to describe that which I think I saw.

Rat-like. Greyish. Certainly rat-shaped, the largest not being more than twelve inches long, with a thin snake for a tail. Like those that encumbered the princess's head, but just one – and thin. A thin snake, flesh-coloured, standing in as a rat tail, which seemed to be seeking nourishment from whatever was in its immediate vicinity. Or maybe the quick darting movement was merely an automatic impulse and they did not need nourishment in the way mankind understands that word. But they moved so fast (the rat-like creatures), turning the windows into a vista of a milliard red microscopic eyes that seemed to glow with their own light.

And sitting there next to the princess, I revived the faintest ghost of a memory that had been formed in another place, another time, in another life – when I had been awakened by some movement and had quickly come to understand that one or more of those creatures was in bed with me. I could feel a snake tail round my left ankle.

'Chu-Chu,' the princess was holding me, her arms tight around my person, 'you have been exposed much too early and for too long. Now relax. Helena will look after you. Don't worry – all will be well.'

Gredelsa had slid back half of the glass partition and was looking at me with a somewhat gloating expression.

'That scream really startled me, Madame. You should have insisted he cover his eyes. Now the chances are he'll be of no use to you at all.'

But my lady only hugged me the tighter and spoke words that proved she understood.

'It was not what he saw that made him scream, but what he remembered. Be thankful your memory screen does not record any such experience. And already he has summoned self-control. Is that not so, Chu-Chu?'

The chauffeur's voice sounded very commonplace, like that of an airline pilot announcing the expected time of arrival.

'We will be leaving the time mist in two minutes, Madame.'

'Splendid, it will be so nice to be home again.'

Scarcely had she finished speaking than the darkness beyond the car windows swiftly took on the aspect of gloomy twilight and I looked out upon dense woods that flanked either side of the road, where leafless black trees interlocked skeletal branches and fantastic shadows took on grotesque shapes such as he who has been jilted by sleep sees dancing on the ceiling when a boisterous wind is chasing clouds across a moonlit sky. But I could not determine if it was night or day for what light there was came filtered through the overhead branches and could have originated either from a cloud-veiled sun or the cold glory of a full moon.

The princess patted my hand and said in the voice one uses to pacify a frightened child:

'It's all right, Chu-Chu, soon we'll be out of Desolation Woods and then there will be light, then we will be happy again. For is not light a reflection sent out by the sea of life and can never for long be masked by darkness?'

'Then what is darkness?' I asked still watching the swiftly passing woods which were at least moving in the traditional direction. 'I've often wondered.'

'Light is positive,' the princess replied, 'because it exists. Darkness is negative as it only owes its existence to the absence of light. Therefore darkness does not exist. Neither does time and space.'

I was in no mood to take part in a rather senseless debate for the depressing woods were being left behind and replaced by fairly normal countryside where brown and white cows browsed placidly in lush fields and a wide stream wended its way towards a range of distant hills.

'Come through the time mists, Madame,' the chauffeur announced.

'Obviously,' the princess retorted with some impatience. 'Now put your foot down. My Chu-Chu is famished. Is that not so, my precious?'

I, who up to that time had assumed it would be a long time before I thought of food again, suddenly realised I was very hungry, so much so there was a distinct weakness in the area of my knees, reminding me of the time when – the result of circumstances there is no need to mention here – I had not eaten for three entire days. Not for the first time the princess appeared to have tuned in on my thoughts, for she said: 'Passing through the time mist does rather confuse one's personal time illusion for I have known extreme cases where a traveller has emerged suffering from malnutrition.'

The car swung round smoothly into a drive which was guarded by two immense iron gates – which were wide open – flanked by tall trees and continued onward for some one and a half miles until we came to a large house that might well have grown from the ground on which it stood.

It was a large timeless house, there being no part of it that I could recognize as belonging to any particular period. Rather, it appeared to have a period all of its own.

There was more than a suggestion of triangles, originating from several gable roofs, but even so the deep-set windows appeared to be made up of three or more triangles even though they were distinctly rectangular in shape. The same could be said of the massive oak doors which were protected by a deep porch equipped with three stone pillars supporting a gable roof.

The house appeared to be built of large granite blocks or some material surfaced to look like granite and all the stonework, windows, guttering, seemed to be new. In fact the builders could have departed only yesterday, or maybe I was only permitted to see that part which they had just completed and they were still toiling away somewhere out of sight, probably at the back. Later I was to discover this was not so but even then the impression still remained.

The car drew up at three black marble steps, but before it had stopped, two footmen, looking very flustered as though we had arrived unawares, wearing black velvet jackets, grey satin shirts and bright red knee breeches, ran down the steps, one to open the near side door, the other the far side. I noticed the one who insisted on helping me down had an untidily tied cravat and a white wig that had slipped over one ear.

The princess ordered quietly: 'Take charge, Gredelsa.'

This the maid did with more pleasure than I had yet seen her demonstrate, for a gloating smile transformed her face into the likeness of a satyrical mask and a gleam in her eyes that boded ill for anyone who found themselves in her power. She disappeared into the house where briefly I could hear her shouting threats and orders. The princess smiled gently as she steered me towards the front doorway. 'Gredelsa loves to play at make-believe.'

We entered a commodious hall where a number of young maid-servants attired in long black dresses relieved by small white aprons and tiny lace caps, were sweeping, brushing – and in one place – scrubbing. The entire place recreated the impression I had wandered into one of the more fantastic scenes from *Alice Through the Looking Glass.*

And Gredelsa seemed to fling herself into this mad activity like a fury mounted on a whirlwind, producing mops, brooms, brushes from a cupboard under the stairs, pushing them into hands that up to that time had only gripped a duster or nothing at all, so that the amount of brushing, sweeping and running about became more intensified. Just as it was about to become overwhelming, the princess lightly brushed her fingers across my forehead and said gently:

'You must not allow Far Acres to play havoc with imagination, Chu-Chu. Now, close your eyes – that's right – say to yourself – I will see true – good. Now open your eyes.'

When I next looked upon the spacious hall it was to see one or two maids more soberly dressed giving the last finishing touches to a well-brushed, swept and polished room.

Gredelsa barked: 'Kitchen!' and disappeared round a corner.

The princess slid a hand over my arm.

'What a clever Chu-Chu he is! Given an inch and he'll step forward one mile. How quickly you dismissed the fantastic and adopted the commonplace. More and more I appreciate the happy chance which brought us together. Now follow me and I will show you your room.'

Wooden stairs supported by black marble balusters. Walls covered by orange-black-streaked paper, all dimly lit by windows with small black and white panes. I thought Madame's wig stirred uneasily as she mounted the stairs and I became aware of a cold draught when we came up on to the first landing; a real shiver-maker such as one experiences when old floorboards are removed and a cold stale current of air escapes to assault the senses and arouse the sleeping dogs of memory.

The room she ushered me into was comfortable and neat being furnished by a double divan, walnut wardrobe, chest of drawers and two armchairs. A fitted red carpet covered the floor.

A monstrous brown rat sat on a chest of drawers preening its fur.

The princess giggled like an excited schoolgirl.

'Get rid of it,' she said.

'You mean. . .?'

'Just get rid of it. The house is trying to play tricks.'

The rat after giving us one enquiring glance began to lick its paws. Had it been a white rat I would have thought it to be rather endearing. Strange how colour made all that difference.

'Well?' the princess enquired.

'Go away,' I ordered the rat. 'Shoo!'

The brown rat instantly changed into a marmalade cat that was in the act of washing its face.

'What is the name of this house?' I asked.

'I thought you knew. Far Acres.'

I thought deeply for some while then said – not really understanding what I really meant: 'I thought that somewhere – sometime – it had a different name.'

The princess shrugged. 'It has I believe had many names in the minds of those who see and hear more than is comfortable. Now I will leave you. When you feel hungry a gong will sound, then you must come downstairs to what will be then the dining-room and partake.'

I waited until she was about to close the door before enquiring: 'Where did the cat go?'

She replied without turning her head. 'You didn't really want it – did you?'

That seemed to be a reasonable answer so I murmured: 'Thank you,' as the door closed.

*

There could be no doubt that the land beyond the time mist, Far Acres, was having a strange effect on me, for I could not from one minute to the next be certain what I was eating in the dining-room. Grilled steak changed into roast pork during the short period it took to raise fork to mouth, then became braised kidneys before I had time to ask my lady to explain this phenomenon.

'You will experience strange things during the adjustment

period,' she tried to explain. 'Remember the rat and the cat? Now it's boiled or baked potatoes, grilled steak and roast pork. In fact you are eating a yeast-vegetable compound that will eventually taste like roast lamb. That is of course taking into consideration the fact that you may not be eating anything at all.'

Normally I would have assumed my leg was being pulled to an enormous length, but having accepted Madame's own unique state of being, plus that which I had seen and experienced so far, I was by now conditioned to believe absolutely anything.

'What will happen when I'm fully adjusted?'

'You will see what all super-normal people see and even occasionally that which super-abnormal people do not see.'

I plucked a leaf from the tree of knowledge.

'Then I will know the difference between good and evil?'

Her lips parted as an enigmatic smile. 'Say the difference between right and wrong. Evil is only an anagram for live or vile. Good is meaningless.'

She filled two green wine glasses and slid one over the table to me. As I sipped the golden liquid, I realised that nectar is not sweet, but bitter like gall; its effect on the brain was to clear it of all waste thought, wiping the slate of memory clean so that experience could begin a fresh chapter.

'Are you prepared to pay homage to a strange god?' she enquired.

'I will pay for knowledge in any coin you wish,' I replied.

'Then drink your nasty wine, eat your pears in apple juice, then wait for Gredelsa to serve strong black coffee enriched by wild honey.'

'Honey in coffee?'

'Coffee like sin should be hot, black and exceedingly sweet.'

'Is sin right or wrong?'

'Neither. Or both. Without sin you cannot ask for forgiveness.'

'I wonder what it is like to be sinless?'

She shook her head as though trying to dislodge an unpleasant memory. 'Once I tried to live without sin – and do you know what happened?'

'You committed the ultimate sin – by being sinless.'

A hint of anger lit her eyes and her voice took on a steel like undertone.

'Clever. Oh, very clever. Remember evil is the anagram of live, but evil is also the food of genius.'

'Then sin is right?'

'Add four more letters and you have sincere.'

'But those four letters can be identified with death. Cere. As in cerecloth. Winding sheet.'

The princess got up and pushed back her chair.

'You are becoming exceedingly mournful, Chu-Chu. Finish eating and drinking what you think you are eating and drinking, then join me in the hall. I would like you to see the rest of the house, an experience that should at least waken the sleeping memories in your brain.'

I pushed back my chair. 'I have dined more than enough.'

As we left the room, I glanced at Gredelsa who must now be regarded as a friend and noticed with some gratification the former look of contempt had been replaced by one of regard. We went back to the large hall where there was not a single servant in sight, although I was convinced it would only take a snap of the fingers for them silently to emerge from behind closed doors. But as though to disprove this supposition the princess began to open doors, revealing rooms that were decorated and furnished in dominant colours. She allowed me a quick look, snapped: 'Green drawing room,' then slammed the door before opening the next. I counted three drawing rooms, each preceded by its colour, one lounge, one library, one music room (but no sign of a musical instrument), and it must be confessed I was not all that surprised when I, prompted by some impulse, opened one door immediately after the princess had closed it, only to find the room had changed its decor within the last five seconds. Madame noticed my action and wagged her forefinger at me.

'That was a very naughty thing to do. You might have taken the room by surprise and seen something very nasty indeed. Don't over-strain your self-control and mental energy. Given time the unusual will become normal and you will have no occasion to experience alarm or even fear. Remember familiarity is the great leveller. Sit in a roaring fire for a thousand years and you'll get used to it.'

'True, Madame, but a thousand years is a long time.'

'Not if you're doomed to live for ever it isn't. But enough of this pointless discussion and house viewing. I will take you to the temple and there you can acquire food for thought.'

We left the house by a back entrance and walked through a magnificent flower garden where a preponderance of blended perfumes momentarily made my head swim; reviving memories of a long ago childhood and a beautiful grey-haired lady who wept because of a fatal journey I was about to undertake.

The princess nudged me. 'Do not persist in looking back. It's an energy-wasting practice.'

A tall red-bricked building stood just beyond the garden, surrounded by an expanse of red-cement paving, that in turn was confined by gilt-painted railings. The building had a flat roof from which rose an immense gold-plated (as I later was so informed) cobra, its hood fully dilated.

The effect was both amazing and awe-inspiring, for an observer might be forgiven for supposing the main body of the reptile was down in the building and only the immense head visible.

'The Golden Serpent,' the princess murmured. 'Netjer-Ankh. The living god. One of the minor divinities of ancient Egypt, but of great power notwithstanding.' She sighed deeply. 'One whom it was disastrous to offend.'

She opened a small gate set in the gilt railings and preceded me across the expanse of red cement (so I had supposed it to be) until we came to two giant bronze doors; one opened when the princess lightly touched a small gold knob, to reveal a fabulously decorated interior.

To begin – it was much larger than the exterior – large as that was – even suggested. I have since come to understand this was the result of a close proximity of two dimensions, which may have been why the temple although windowless, was brilliantly lit by a mysterious light source that seemed to radiate from the high ceiling.

The walls were covered with what I assumed to be alternate gold and silver tiles, each about a foot square and enhanced by a large ruby or emerald set in the centre. The floor was covered or made from what appeared to be green-tinted mirror glass, only now I suspect it wasn't glass but some kind of metal or alloy, and this reflected the light that originated from the ceiling and gave the impression I was about to walk through silver fire.

'Stay here forever and you will live forever,' the princess whispered.

At the far end, and how far away that seemed, stood an altar. Built of gold – or some even more precious metal – bricks, a vast rectangular block with a gold cobra coiled on its surface, its extended hood serving as a backcloth for the glittering rubies that were its eyes. On the front of the altar was embossed in alternate rubies and emeralds the old name for the living snake god:

NETJER-ANKH

Princess Helena took my arm and urged me across the mirror floor, through the reflected light that seemed like silver-illuminated mist that entered my body by means of the five openings and finally flooded my brain. The result was exhilarating and rather alarming, for it seemed as if liquid fire was pouring through my veins and those parts of my brain that up to that time I had no reason to suppose even existed was suddenly throbbing with a kind of alien life.

'Damp down the fire,' the princess instructed, 'regain control. You must expect strange experiences from now on and learn how to cope with them. Now, remount the throne of reason.'

I understood what she meant even if I could not translate that knowledge into words – audible words and sentences are a very poor means of communication – and rapidly damped down the liquid fire and restored my brain into a semblance of the original self.

But, gentlemen, I must warn you, perhaps for the first time, I can no longer be regarded as a normal human being. Smile if you wish, but I speak no less than the absolute truth, as time will prove.

By the time we had crossed the mirror floor and arrived at the golden altar I was more or less prepared for an unusual occurrence, which was just as well, for when the princess sank to her knees – an action I thought it wise to emulate – a voice began as a whisper from somewhere near the ceiling, but presently filled the entire temple.

Now here is the remarkable, even miraculous, fact: although I knew the voice spoke in a language I could not remember hearing before, possibly that used by the hierarchy of Ancient Egypt, I could understand every word.

First it whispered a name, a strange name such as a sleeper may hear when preparing to resume the chains of flesh. Perhaps it first took on voice sound when the primitive life force that was purely masculine began to develop a more gentler aspect that was entirely feminine. It was born of pain, anguish and joy and it came to represent the essence of womanhood; the eternal wife-mistress-mother-protector who still watches over those princes of light who have been condemned to walk the halls of hell-earth for a period that cannot be measured by time.

The name was *Asherian*.

It began as a whisper and gradually grew into a shouted demand:

'Asherian . . . Asherian . . . *Asherian*. . .'

And Princess Helena began to cry. Terrible harsh sobbing cries that shook her body and made the red curls of her monstrous wig tremble – indeed caused it to slip until I had another glimpse of the writhing creatures that were part of her flesh vessel, the living symbol of a curse placed upon her by . . . by what?

The voice, sexless but creating a mental image of a woman-man, took on a more gentle tone, drew a word picture that became a vivid drama in my over-active brain.

'Cursed by a god for a sin that is rarely forgiven, why have you approached my altar? You know the white horse of hope gallops in only one direction. Endure! There is no comfort I can offer you.'

The princess spoke with the voice of a repentant child.

'Answer but one question, mighty Netjer – have I found the one? Is this the mortal who will cause the curse to be lifted?'

When the voice next spoke it was fainter, appeared to be drawing away into an immeasurable distance.

'The future is a white sheet waiting for time to record the

past. But there is the smell of fear about him which will have to be overcome when he comes to the red river. Farewell once Lady of the Shrines, I will not look upon your face again unless it be in anger.'

The voice faded away completely and Princess Helena stood up and wiped her eyes and after gazing upon me for sometime said:

'Rise, Chu-Chu. You must suffice for I have not found anyone that is remotely of your stature and with you therefore I must either sink or swim. But never forget your fate and mine are now irrevocably interwoven and I must follow you through the double doorway. But tell me, how do you feel since entering the temple?'

It was a strange question to ask at that time, but I gave it my full consideration:

'I feel mentally disturbed but physically well. Better than at any time in my life.'

She nodded. 'You have already contracted the only disease that will ever bother you. Immortality.'

In my blissful ignorance I was able to conjure up a chuckle. 'That's impossible for death is needed to allow evolution to bring life to its ultimate goal.'

She gripped my arm and began to lead me back to the doorway. 'Your wisdom is not after all drawn from a bottomless well, Chu-Chu, for immortality is not natural and death is a myth for nothing or anyone really dies and, most important, there is no ultimate goal. Life will continue to evolve for all time. Therefore immortality is a curse because your ego will never evolve. It will remain unaltered amid a universe that is in a condition of continuous change. Even the gods had to adapt and become so changed their original worshippers would never recognize them. In fact if they ever look back to that period which is wrongly called the beginning, it is doubtful if they would recognize themselves.'

The doorway drew nearer and I could see the flower garden that lay beyond, but strangely the sunlight did not enter this awe-inspiring building. I asked one more question.

'Who – what are the immortal gods?'

The princess shook her head and now clasped my arm with both hands.

'How can I explain, Chu-Chu, to you who have yet to learn why a caterpillar takes a long journey along a blade of grass? They came into being when the great ball of life exploded and its fragments went hurtling across the awful abyss of nothing which had never existed. I suppose you could say they were the first symbols of intelligent life and early man looked to them for protection and guidance – but rarely got it, for their main function is to promote growth and destroy all that which does not contribute to that purpose. The fate of billions is not important and not one divine tear will be shed if they all perish miserably in a slow burning fire.'

It is possible she would have told me more, although I had understood little and believed even less of what I had so far been told, when we stepped out into the sunlight where bees hummed the song of summer and a warm breeze caressed my face and almost everything I had heard and seen in the temple slipped back into a semi-mist of not-to-be-remembered, although the feeling of well-being remained.

In silence we walked back to the house, but on the way I became conscious of the fact that none of the colourful flowers belonged to any species I could recognize. The same could be said for the giant butterflies that ranged in colour from bright orange to vivid green. Another point that gradually registered on my consciousness was the pink sky that contrasted nicely with light blue clouds. I drew the princess's attention to this but she merely shrugged.

'You are looking at a different universe through an alien atmosphere,' she explained with some impatience as though the colour of sky and clouds was a matter of little importance.

When we re-entered the house we were met by a grim-faced Gredelsa who addressed the princess with scant ceremony.

'Madame, your weekly treatment is long overdue, so if you'll go to your room I'll be along directly.'

Both looked at me with a kind of blood chilling enquiry until the princess asked:

'Do you think it is time for Chu-Chu to watch the treatment being applied? Even possibly help you?'

Gredelsa made a hideous face. 'Why not, Madame? Either he has begun to adapt or he never will. If he should prove to be a failure here at Far Acres, he will never. . .'

She did not finish the sentence and the princess nodded even while she stroked my cheek.

'Indeed that is true. Chu-Chu, you are going to take an important step forward – watch the treatment. In a way you are very unique for no one before you has ever got this far. But first let us dine for I cannot face the razor on an empty stomach. No, Gredelsa, the dining room first, the bedroom afterwards.'

I, who remembered the meal we had eaten but a short time ago, would have argued, but the princess shook her head impatiently.

'You are exceedingly hungry again, Chu-Chu, you know you are. Take my arm and we will go in together. Gredelsa eats with us on this occasion.'

By the time she had finished speaking my stomach did feel as if it had not been filled for at least three days even though I had little inclination for food. I have since come to the conclusion that there were several time dimensions at Far Acres and they most possibly over-lapped in the temple; receded when voice spoke, which resulted in a move forward of several hours when we stepped out into the sunlight again.

There may have been another explanation, but Helena (or Asherian) either could not or would not unravel the mystery for me, in fact seemed to derive a mischievous satisfaction from my confusion.

Now in retrospect I realise the second meal in the dining room was in every respect a duplicate of the first; indeed *it could have been the same meal eaten for the second time*. Yet the conversation varied for the simple reason both the princess and I made an effort to make it so.

Presently she burst into a fit of hysterical laughter and ran from the room. Gredelsa looked at me with something akin to regard and pity.

'Go take a little walk,' she advised. 'Gather strength.'

CHAPTER FOUR

I left the dining-room, walked the corridors and did not allow my brain to register everything I saw, heard or touched. I do remember meeting a very pretty girl with red-gold hair; a lovely creature who wore an off-the-shoulder red dress and looked at me with a shy smile. I believe we spoke for a little while, but I cannot remember what we said. But I do know her face and voice were familiar and bitter-sweet memories were aroused from their long sleep particularly when her brilliant dark eyes looked into mine.

The entire experience was like being three-quarters drunk, the state when the bemused brain is trying to equate fantasy with reality and ends up blending the two. Then Gredelsa was standing in front of me, saying in a harsh cold voice:

'Now . . . now is the testing time.'

And I was wide awake and sober as a sinful man on judgement day.

*

The princess was sitting up in her vast bed, her head covered by a beautiful cashmere shawl. She patted the bed and motioned for me to sit beside her. When I had done so she took hold of my left hand and kissed it gently, then looking up at me with a hint of tears in her eyes she said:

'Chu-Chu, I want you to be very brave and do exactly what I tell you. Remember that fear is the only enemy and once it has been faced you will be established as captain of your body and soul. And, Chu-Chu, also realise this. Your ego, *AM*, has unlimited power. It can perform so-called miracles, erase and create, for it is a fraction of the whole and the whole is life indivisible.'

'What are you trying to tell me?' I asked.

'That in a short while fear will appear in a terrible guise and you must take it by the throat and strangle it. Then the power will flare up and enable you to work a so-called miracle. Will you do what I ask?'

'I will try.'

'That's no good, suggesting as it does you are prepared to fail. Say with conviction: I will.'

'I will.'

'Good.' She looked at Gredelsa and nodded. 'There's no point in further delay. Do what must be done.'

'Without delay, Madame the Princess.'

She was as good as her word. The shawl was pulled from the princess's head and the entire hideous crop revealed. They hissed, writhed, fought among themselves and looked much as when I had uncovered them the night before. With a slight exception. They had grown longer. In particular the thick ones at the base of the skull which now all but covered the nape of the neck, while those on either side, now free from the confining folds of the shawl, flopped down over the ears and swayed back and forth in an apparent effort to reach the chin.

Gredelsa took two pairs of thick rubber gloves and after handing one pair to me, began to draw on the other pair over her own large hands. She gave me an unblinking stare.

'They must be trimmed down, otherwise no shawl or wig will hide them. They can grow to a very long length – below Madame's waist. We will cut them.'

'Cut them!'

She made an abrupt impatient gesture. 'Yes, cut them to half an inch of Madame's skull. The shorter the better then long time before another haircut.'

I could only stare with dilated eyes at the row of cut-throat razors that were laid out neatly on a towel and the yellow plastic bowl that Gredelsa placed on the bed. She took up one razor and began to hone it on a leather strop that was fitted to the bedside cabinet. Indeed there was no hesitation.

'Hold Madame's head,' she ordered. 'Place your hand under her chin and grip tightly. Do not be afraid they cannot bite through the thick gloves. But keep head still.'

The princess looked up at me when I slid a reluctant hand under her chin and her eyes smiled. Gredelsa plunged her fingers into the writhing mass of coils and pulled out one long monster that had hidden its full length among its fellows, then after wrapping it three times round her hand, applied the razor.

The princess screamed and drummed her feet on the bottom of the bed, while I held her head as still as I could, doing my very best neither to look into her eyes or take any notice of what Gredelsa was doing to her head. She snarled at me.

'Cut it up.'

'Cut. . .?'

'The long one on bed. Get out of bowl. Cut into small pieces.'

I looked down and saw she was half right. The first very long one she had cut off was almost over the bowl rim, leaving a thin trail of blood as it made its bid for freedom.

'Use both hands,' Gredelsa ordered. 'I will not amputate further until you finish. And hurry, Madame wants me to end quickly.'

I picked the awful thing up by finger and thumb and instantly the jaws spat green foam but the thick gloves protected my hand, then dropped it back into the bowl where I managed to carve it into small portions with a razor. The portions continued to wriggle for some time.

'If you are to be sick, not over the bed,' Gredelsa instructed. 'Now hold Madame's head tight for I am about to cut the first bunch. It better that way, much quicker.'

Again plunging her fingers into the writhing mass she gathered five into a bunch and skilfully sliced them off close to the root. Madame released a long drawn-out shriek and all but jerked her head from my grip, but somehow I hung on while nerving myself to watch the maid's tonsorial operation.

She worked with great speed, never cutting more than six at one time, less with the thick ones at the rear and I was surprised to see that the bowl was three-quarters full of wriggling lengths when she had only half completed her task. The stumps clotted almost at once and there was very little seepage, and I was fascinated to see (damnable curiosity again) those that had been cut first had already acquired a thin protective skin. When the princess's head was a mass of red stumps save for a still very active patch at the very front, Gredelsa handed me her razor and said:

'Finish off. Show Madame you can manage if I'm not here.'

I would have refused but the princess's weak, tremulous voice whispered:

'Strangle fear . . . you said . . . I will.'

My stomach had been kept under control, I had cut one squirming thing into small pieces, I had watched Gredelsa perform her ghastly work – cutting them off myself should not prove to be an impossible task.

I accepted the blood-stained razor, gathered up the writhing, softly squelching things into a tight bunch and cut neatly a fraction of an inch above the scalp. I quickly dropped my harvest into the bowl, which was now filled to the brim.

After Geredelsa had covered the princess's lacerated head with tightly bound bandages, Madame gave me a weak smile and insisted on kissing me.

'Good boy. You have done very well, hasn't he, Gredelsa?'

'With practice he *should* do very well,' Gredelsa agreed with obvious reservations. 'At least he not sick over the bed or ran away and hide. Now you sleep. We all sleep. But first I get rid of trimmings.'

I turned my head when she carried the over full bowl to the door, but then had to run and open it for her, she not being able to do so herself. When I returned to the bed the princess smiled like a weary child.

'Leave me now, Chu-Chu. If you can't sleep go for a long walk. The air has some wonderful properties here at Far Acres.'

I lost no time in leaving the house and found the air was indeed bracing, reinforcing the feeling of well-being that had first come to me in the temple. The road, grass, trees and occasional house had a new, perfect look, as though they too had just been planted or erected. When I came to one red-tiled, white painted rough cast bungalow I took the trouble to open a white gate and walk up the crazy-paved path, then raise and lower the gleaming brass knocker. After some little while spent in this useless exercise I approached the first bay window and peered through the crystal clear glass pane; all I could see was an impregnable darkness. A property house that fitted very nicely into the surrounding decor, but must not be taken for real. In fact Far Acres itself without any doubt was a realm reflected on the brain, then projected with some semblance to reality.

Curiosity was by now becoming bloated, its appetite more than sated by an over-abundance of acquired knowledge; knowledge that I was attached to this land and its mistress by invisible chains.

The lady had charm and I had the ability to adjust and it did not take much imagination to understand how the next fantasy episode came into being.

I found him standing on a narrow bridge, leaning over a low wall looking down into the quietly flowing stream. He was neither fat or thin, young or all that old, his hair yellow-tinted grey, neither was he handsome or ugly. Attired in grey trousers and lilac-coloured shirt, his feet encased in grey towel socks and Marks & Spencers slippers.

I stood beside him and for a while neither spoke; then he asked: 'You know who I am?'

I thought very carefully for some considerable time; took due note of the black smudge on the back of his left hand, the kind one gets from changing a typing ribbon. There was a red ridge on the top of his nose that suggested he wore spectacles when reading or writing.

'I'd rather not know,' I eventually said.

He spat into the slow-moving stream and watched the little ring of bubbles disappear under the bridge. He spoke more to himself than to me his reluctant audience.

'I try to be feasible. Keep a tight rein on imagination. It can so easily run away with one, can it not?'

I nodded. There was nothing I could say that would make the slightest sense although a cascade of questions threatened to pour off my tongue. He looked up at the sky, then around at the motionless trees, before turning to me. I thought he looked tired and drawn. There was a husky quality about his voice.

'I did my best but all this lacks credibility. But it's the characters, you lot, that are the trouble. I think up some first rate dialogue but you will change it. Think you know best. The plot – well let's face it – is original but somehow it acquires a mundane aspect, then finally I strive for a happy ending. But the chances are one or more of you will commit suicide or murder someone or finish up as a wailing phantom.'

'You made us,' I replied not really understanding what I was saying.

'Such is the popular misconception.' He waved his hand in a gesture that embraced the surrounding countryside. 'I suppose all this is an extension of me, in the same way the princess's snakes are an extension of her, but, damn me hide, I gave birth to the lot. Then why isn't my will supreme?'

'Few children do what their parents tell them,' I murmured.

'At least they don't take the house over and tell their creators what to do.'

I left him leaning over the wall looking mournfully down into the stream: when I was some hundred yards further on he called after me:

'You – whatsyourname – you do realise I can wipe this lot out, all of you, by a single thought? I mean, if I am who you think I am, I should have done that long ago. Wipe the slate, or word processor, clean. Begin all over again.'

I broke into a run and did not stop until I reached the house – the house with the Rolls standing outside – and I could take an illusionary refuge inside.

I went to my room and lying down on the bed covered my head with a blanket and imagined I was a child again, hiding from the awful black shape that came from the fireplace.

*

Days passed – or light grew bright then faded again but no one in Far Acres grew any older. And I was in daily and nightly attendance on Madame the Princess.

Familiarity does indeed breed – if not contempt – at least self-confidence. Or perhaps understanding and a measure of compassion.

I looked upon the horror that was Helena's head and began to imagine – I am after all a professional imaginer – what it must be like to have a head of snakes. Not to comb hair, but trim snakes. Or whatever those things were. I am still of the opinion they were a species of maggot, possibly first brought into being by a virus injected into the bloodstream. There is no such phenomenon as the supernatural, as any experience witnessed by the senses must be the result of some natural law.

But I need hardly say, gentlemen, I still had a lot to learn. I still have regardless of my exalted position, but already my ignorance has been diluted to an alarming degree and there is a kind of knowledge that multiplies and eventually feeds upon the sanity of its host. If this has become my fate I must leave it to you to decide.

There had been talk of an antidote but I had never been invited to take advantage of it, so I had decided it was the result of wishful thinking. Gredelsa hinted on more than one occasion that she had become infected and surely she would have been protected if that were at all possible. And Madame the Princess herself?

Even I could see over the ensuing days the condition was getting worse. Red boil-like protuberances were appearing on the nape of her neck and even the suggestion of one on the right shoulder. I did not dare ask the question that was uppermost in my mind, but the princess as always seemed capable of reading my thoughts for she said softly:

'I do not know, Chu-Chu, but I think it quite possible that I may have to become more hideous, repulsive, than I am now before the final test can be effective. But those on the neck and shoulder – hot poultices have in the past dispersed them, though not anymore it would seem.'

While she spoke her head lay motionless on the pillow and the crop remained still also, with just one length slithering to a more comfortable position and I wondered what effect drugs would have on them. Instantly the princess enlightened me.

'Chu-Chu, my body has become accustomed to the most powerful drug and robbed me of any kind of assisted sleep.'

The *word* flashed across my brain but was at once extinguished when the princess sent out a blast of anger.

'Do you not think I would have welcomed death long ago had his Dark Majesty been allowed to approach me? The curse and immortality are twin diseases that time can never cure. But never mind that now.'

And she shook her head impatiently which had the immediate effect of making the entire crop rear up, open minute jaws and hiss in unison.

'Put on a glove and soothe them,' the princess all but pleaded, 'I would like you to get used to rendering this little service. The glove is there and it will fit your elegant hand. You have worn it before. Remember the last trimming.' She released another deep sigh. 'They grow so quickly, and the cutting is so painful.'

Courage can only be measured by the yardstick of will-power. I slid my right hand into the thickly padded glove, then willed myself to lower it down into that hissing, writhing mass.

I tried to imagine it was like stroking a cat, and wasn't all that successful. There could be no doubt that several did try to bite me, for they unlocked their jaws and attempted to drive minute fangs into the thickness of the glove and these futile acts caused the princess to gasp several times then mutter:

'Hurry, Chu-Chu, quieten them down. Quickly. . .'

It took me many stomach-heaving minutes to get my fingers down among the short stubby bodies – for they were not yet fully grown – and sort of tickle them. One that was a little thinner and longer than the rest, coiled round my index finger and when I tried to pull free the princess screamed, making me realise that the roots must be quite deep and connected with her nerve grid. The agony she must suffer when they were being trimmed could not be imagined and I dreaded the prospect of having to assist at that operation again.

'Do not think about it,' the princess murmured. 'Just keep your fingers slightly curved and then there is less chance of one or more coiling round them. But now twist your finger anti-clockwise and gently ease it free. That's right. . . But I think that is enough for the time being. Later on today you can come back and comfort me again.'

As always, I was relieved to leave her although lately an element of pity made me wish I could do more to help her. Also, having settled in I had begun to investigate both the house and the staff who ran it. The house like its surroundings gave the impression it was new; furniture and carpets seemed to have come recently from a brand-new factory and even a streak of dust I found on a window ledge was – how can I explain? – was clean, having been ejected from a new dust dispenser, its sole purpose to complete a well-lived in decor.

The staff were another matter entirely. I experienced great difficulty in tracking them down, despite the fact they were always to hand when needed.

For example, when I failed to find a clean towel in the airing cupboard, I had only to turn to find a pretty maid with six various coloured towels draped over her left arm, but when I tried to engage her in conversation she somehow disappeared in the shower cubicle. I know that does not seem possible, but it's true. She seemed suddenly to match the flower pattern plastic curtain, then merge into it, but when I opened the bathroom door there she was walking demurely down the passage.

The same kind of thing took place at meal-times. Two maids and a footman waited on table, but I swear if you took your eye off them they did not so much disappear as not be there. Gredelsa made a great business of chasing the staff and ensuring they kept the place clean, but as I have already stated it was necessary to distribute phoney dirt to create the illusion the place needed cleaning.

I found the kitchen after a lot of corner-turning and door-opening and when I finally succeeded in following my nose and stepped into a large stone-paved room where saucepans rattled lids on stainless steel hotplates it took an effort to remember when I stood immediately outside the door there was no sound whatsoever.

The chauffeur was real enough but might have been dumb for all the information I managed to get out of him. He had a way of touching his cap which served as an answer to any question I put to him. It even seemed to be some kind of sign language that might make sense if translated to a yet to be revealed formula.

The dark woman I had first seen in the hotel bar put in an appearance. I spotted her strolling round the elaborate flower garden and was not surprised when she instantly transported herself from the paved path to a smooth patch of lawn surrounding several flower beds. I did not attempt to pursue her.

Orange clouds drifted across the pink sky, but nowhere did I see the slightest sign of a sun, even though a pale disc of white light which remained poised just over the furthermost trees could have been a moon. Once I had to take shelter in a flower-covered bower when a shower of purple rain formed enchanting puddles on the paths and had the temporary effect of turning the grass bright blue. As though sprinkled with dye or rinsing water.

Measuring time was almost an impossibility as there were no clocks in the house and no change in the light outside, but according to my wrist watch I had been two days in Far Acres when Katrina put in appearance.

I found her in the same bower in which I had taken shelter against the shower, seated on a rustic seat which I could not remember seeing before, dressed in a white muslin dress with a matching ribbon that confined her hair into a long pony tail. She looked young, extremely pretty and vulnerable. She greeted me with a shy smile and looked up from under long lashes. Her soft voice had a lilting quality.

'Hullo! Who are you?'

'I'm Gore Sinclair.'

She pretended to shudder. 'Gore! Blood! You must be the friend that Madame the Princess has brought with her. Does she not call you Chu-Chu?'

'Yes, and I don't like it.'

She nodded and stared at me with deep blue eyes when I seated myself beside her. 'Yes, she is not always kind, having had her own way for such a long time she assumes her whims and wishes are everyone's pleasure.'

I frowned. 'I'm not sure if I fully understand that.'

She made a charming little grimace. 'I know. Sometimes I am very difficult to understand. But I haven't introduced myself. I am Katrina Landi. A sort of niece to the princess. You . . . what would you like me to call you?'

'My second name is Stephen.'

'I like that. Now we've been properly introduced. And one day we'll be old friends. Isn't that nice?'

'I'd rather be your young friend. Old is a nasty word.'

She released her breath as a gasp of protest. 'But it isn't. Old is a comforting word. Old is the knocker fitted to the door of life which Death uses when he pays his one visit. Old is mellow, kind, gentle. . . But let us talk of other things. Do you like Far Acres?'

'I think so. It takes a bit of getting used to.'

'Doesn't it though? And me? Do you think I'm pretty?'

'Most certainly yes. I'm not at all sure you aren't beautiful.'

She put her head on to one side and appeared to be lost in thought for some time, before saying with a most serious air:

'That's very profound of you. But can we agree that I have the promise of great beauty which will come to full bloom when I decide to come of age? Are you in love with me yet?'

The question was in the nature of a body blow and it took me a little while to think up a suitable answer. 'Well, we've only just met and I can't really make up my mind about such an important issue straightaway.'

She nodded again but this time most vigorously. 'That is very wise. But I expect you will soon be – in love with me. And I'll absolutely adore you. That's the way the plot goes, doesn't it? I don't suppose we'll get married or anything like that. A dark melancholy fate would be rather lovely, don't you think? If I could die in your arms while murmuring words of. . .'

'You are being both childish and silly,' I interrupted and was completely unmanned when tears appeared in her lovely eyes.

'You are so right. But I can't help it. I seem to be made for saccharine and tinsel romances. I sort of go with the trees, flowers and coloured rain. But I am real. As real as hot-cross buns on Good Friday.'

'I'm sure of that. And some people can be childish and silly in the most enchanting way. So – please don't cry.'

'Have you got a handkerchief? A nice big one?'

I took a large red handkerchief from my breast pocket and after flapping it open, gave it to her. She wiped her eyes, blew her nose, then returned the handkerchief.

'You are indeed very kind and already I like you very much, which is a promising beginning to a tender relationship. Will you come to see me often?'

'I will . . . indeed I will. And can I call you Katrina?'

'You must certainly never call me Miss, Madam or Lady Landi, and you will always be Stephen – to me.'

A piece of completely trivial information insisted on slipping off my tongue. 'I had an ancestor who was Sir Stephen Sinclair and he came to a dreadful end?'*

Her lips were transformed into a perfect red circle. 'Really! What kind of dreadful end?'

'I think he was drawn into a wall and partly digested.'

* See *Tales from the Hidden World.*

'How simply dreadful! Well, that will never happen to you. And in any case you're not a sir – are you?'

'No. I'm just a grey sheep of a black family. Must you go now?'

She edged a little nearer and with a child-like simplicity kissed me on the cheek. 'I must. Oh yes. I must go or that horrible Gredelsa will start worrying.'

'Gredelsa! What has she to do with you?'

'Oh, she looks after me. Well, there's no one else.'

I tried to grab her, draw her into my arms, but she slid back along the seat, then rose and ran swiftly down one of the paths. She turned and waved before disappearing from my sight.

Back at the house I tracked Gredelsa down to the airing room and there watched her iron small napkins with a steam iron before placing them in a black wooden box which had a large white X painted on each end.

I waited in vain for her to speak, so eventually asked:

'Who is Katrina? And where do you keep her?'

She froze and kept absolutely still, the iron some half an inch above the ironing board. Presently she asked:

'Where did you see that . . . that young lady?'

'In the bower. About ten minutes ago. She said you looked after her.'

The iron was lowered very gently on to a napkin and the slow movement back and forth continued. Then Gredelsa said:

'Yes, I look after her to the very best of my ability. But be careful, do not under any circumstances encourage her. That is to say, go looking for her.'

I frowned and tried to remember something my instinct told me I should never have forgotten. Instead I asked that short, terrible and most asked question: 'Why?'

Gredelsa seemed to have difficulty in thinking up an answer to my brief question, until she gave a most unsatisfactory one:

'Because it might not be wise to do so.'

I had no recourse other than to repeat the terrible brief question.

'Why?'

'Because that is the way it must be. Now, do not question me further, and do not seek or look for the Lady Katrina. What is that mark on your cheek?'

I rubbed my left cheek but could feel nothing, then seeing the shining surface of the steam iron, peered down at my reflection. There was a red mark on my left cheek such as might be made by a pair of lips wearing non-kissproof lipstick. But rub as I might it would not go away. Gredelsa stared at me with something akin to horror.

'Well? How did it come there?'

'She, Katrina, kissed me on the cheek.'

She crossed herself with the X sign: left shoulder to right hip, right shoulder to left hip, then muttered something I could not understand. With sudden alarm I examined the mark again.

'Will it go away?'

'No. It will never go away, but no one will see it in a short time. You touched her. Must not touch.'

'But,' I protested, 'I did not touch her. She touched me.'

The gaunt head nodded very slowly. 'Aye there's virtue there. And the contact must have been brief.' After releasing a sigh she returned to her ironing. 'What is done is done and only the gods can know the consequences.'

By now I was unashamably frightened and without thinking of what I was doing grabbed her by the arm.

'What's this all about? Why can't that young girl be touched or be allowed to touch anyone else?'

She did not answer until I had released her arm, then said with exaggerated patience:

'I did not say her ladyship may not touch anyone she chooses. *Allowed* is not a word you use when referring to the Lady Katrina. Neither are submissive words such as: permitted, ordered, refused, instructed, or rebuked, for the Snake God protects even when he punishes.

'But I have spoken far too much. Possibly Madame the Princess will chose to enlighten you in the fullness of time. But I? I can only speak in riddles and advise – and that circumspectly.'

And that was all I could get out of her which resulted in my becoming even more alarmed than before. I decided to approach the princess.

I found her lying on a day-bed in a room that overlooked the rear garden; a colourful view to say the least. She greeted me with a smile and patted a position on the bed which would place me beside her.

'Sit here, Chu-Chu, where I can both see and hear you. Let us amuse ourselves by alternating the view from this window, which is easy to do once you know how.

Almost before she had finished speaking, the garden was hidden under a blanket of snow; a holly tree bright with red berries had replaced the magnolia and a robin red-breast perched on the window sill and looked into the room with bright inquisitive eyes. Where trees had stood at the bottom of the garden two minutes before, there was now a wide open plain across which a solitary horseman was creating a trail of hoof-prints, while gazing up at our window with sad expectancy.

'I wonder,' the princess enquired in a low gentle voice, 'who he can be? How he comes to be alone out there and why he is making for this house? Alas, we may never know for I have no way of finding out if it is the past out here, or the future. It most certainly is not the present. In fact it may just be a picture I have conjured up and projected through your eyes and brain. But now it is your turn. Dream up a new scene.'

I shook my head. 'I couldn't. If that is merely a figment of your imagination then you are a greater dreamer than I will ever be.'

The princess rearranged the shawl over her head and made a tut-tut sound.

'Nonsense. You have been creating your own surroundings all of your conscious life. Reality is only glimpsed when the body sleeps. Come on now, think three ways at once. It's easy.'

It wasn't. Not at first. Then I remembered how in early childhood I had often tried to enter a world where everything was gold and silver. Silver trees with gold leaves, silver grass that was enhanced by gold flowers, the entire scene glittering under a benign silver sky, where a pale gold moon created a soft gentle light.

'Chu-Chu!' The princess released a gasp. 'That is beautiful. Absolutely gorgeous. Who would believe such an artistic soul hid behind so pretty a face. Oh, look! A little gold gazelle has come from behind that gold and silver bush. If ever, Chu-Chu, you realise your full potential, you'll change the face of every known universe. Make another picture. Dip your brush into dream colours.'

For a time a keen pain convulsed my brain, then I exploded into a narrow street with dirt-grimed houses on either side and wet cobble stones beneath my feet. Light was provided by gas street lamps, revealing much I had forgotten existed – in a too easily discovered place.

They stalked the pavements – huge black fur-covered bodies, white expressionless faces that might have been stolen from a dead man who had not lived well or died happy. The eyes were large and black, black as sin-clogged minds, even while they glowed with an inner light that manifest as a single red spark.

Two moons haunted the sky and sparkling stars looked not unlike a mass of polished diamonds cast carelessly on to a sheet of black velvet. I shivered as a cold wind ruffled my hair and a soft voice whispered into my ear:

'Pity these my children so that they may live again.'

And the creatures came soft-footed towards me and one rubbed a wet muzzle against my hand and I shrank back, then turned and ran; slipped, stumbled and finally became painfully aware of gasping breath and pounding heart, even though I had not advanced by so much as an inch.

The voice spoke again. 'If you cannot pity the grotesque how can you hope to love the horrific?'

And when they had completely surrounded me and I could hear the snuffling, feel rough tongues, smell the rank odour, then did self-control collapse and sheer terror usurp the throne of reason.

I did not scream – I shrieked. Instantly the scene trembled, then dissolved and I was back sitting on the princess's day bed; she was passing both hands over my face.

'Now, Chu-Chu, you shouldn't have uncovered such a bleak, dreadful scene. You are not prepared to experience the kind of hell that man has invented.'

She presented me with a black towel and I used it to wipe my forehead, while she dried her hand on a pink bed sheet. Her voice was young and faintly familiar.

'Chu-Chu, I am more and more pleased with you than I have been with anyone else during my very long term of existence. But when you entered the room I formed the opinion you wished to ask me something. Had some burning questions that required answers.'

I nodded although by now I was becoming rather sated with strange information.

'Yes, I have one or two.'

'I hope I can satisfy your curiosity. Unsolved riddles are apt to lead us into a forest of conjecture.'

'Firstly, what, where is Far Acres?'

She gripped one of my hands and shook her head in sad reproach.

'Oh, Chu-Chu! Surely you have guessed the answer to that one? It is a magic land that was created in my brain and given form in yours. And it exists – in so far as it exists at all – in the timeless, limitless void that separates one dimension from another. Anyone can build their fantasy castle and live in it for a thousand years in the time it takes for an eyelid to blink. I know that sounds rather unreal and complicated, but I really can't tell you any more.'

I decided to give the matter much deep thought when I was alone, but in the meanwhile a much more urgent question demanded an answer:

'Who is Katrina?'

'Katrina!'

Instantly the princess was roaring like a tormented lioness. 'Where did you meet that mischief-making, odious, little wretch? Where? Did you seek her out? Did Gredelsa tell you about her? If so she will have reason to curse the day that saw her spawned.'

I trembled for I had never seen her in this state before, or realised she was capable of such a rage. I endeavoured to pacify and explain.

'I found her seated in a bower and passed the time of day. She was very pretty and sweet –'

The princess would not allow me to finish but erupted into an even wilder fit of anger and poured abuse on the young girl I scarcely knew.

'A gigolo who lives off women and now runs after a stupid, conniving little bitch who will be soundly thrashed before very much longer, such a man would not know sweetness were it

given to him in a bowl of sugar. And what did she say about me?
Eh? Mad things no doubt.'

'She only mentioned she was your niece. . .'

A snort interrupted me but I ignored it.

'And Gredelsa looked after her. Otherwise you weren't
mentioned.'

She jerked her head round and the silk shawl slid to one side
and I had a brief glimpse of a tiny snake head before it slid back
into hiding. 'You will have nothing to do with her. Ever.
Understand. If you see her in the grounds – ignore her.'

I reverted to the single three letter question.

'Why?'

'What do you mean why? Because I say so. My wish, word
and whim is the law in Far Acres. That simpering creature will
be suppressed for all time and I will not have you or anyone
encouraging her to defy me.'

There was something obscene about the wet-mouthed
woman whose abuse of a young girl was out of all proportion
to whatever offence – imaginary or real – that may have been
committed. Then her mood changed and I again became very
concerned about possible mishap to the silk shawl. I placed an
arm carefully around her shoulders.

'Please don't upset yourself. I will not see her again if you
would rather I didn't. Not if I can help it at any rate. Please
don't cry.'

She wiped her eyes, blew her nose and spoke more or less
coherently.

'I dread the future – I also wait in vain for it to arrive. . . That
mark on your cheek? She kissed you?'

'She kissed me on the cheek.'

'Love is a destructive emotion. And if I am to be set free, you
have a terrible journey to undergo. And should you look upon
the naked face of the immortal god, then will you have the
power to destroy your own species.'

'I cannot understand how that could happen.'

'The acorn cannot understand how one day it will have
grown into a creation that will tower against the sky. You must
become as the oak tree if I am to be freed from the curse of the
Snake God. But you have another question to ask me.'

I hesitated for a few seconds, then looking her directly in the face I asked:

'Madame the Princess, who are you? And why were you cursed by the Snake God?'

She patted my hand absentmindly before answering.

'Chu-Chu, it is painfully obvious to me I will get no rest until your dreadful curiosity is sated. But I cannot bring myself to relate my strange history and even if I did it is doubtful if you would believe me. Go and look for the library. If you can't find it summon one of the servants and ask the way. Come back when I call you.'

She waved to me as I closed the door.

CHAPTER FIVE

I walked along corridors where white walls were relieved by an occasional gilt-framed picture that mostly depicted views of bleak moorland that seemed to shiver under a snow-filled sky, but nowhere did I come across a servant or any room that looked even remotely like a library.

I had just come to the conclusion I had no great wish to find the library and I might as well look for my own room and take a bath, when the dark woman emerged from round a corner and appeared to make a gesture that could have been translated as an invitation to follow her.

Not so long before I would not have been too happy to do this for her appearance was disquietening to say the least, but by now experience had more or less inured me against being too greatly disturbed by a familiar revenant; so I followed the slim figure through many corridors, down and up innumerable flights of stairs until we came to a long gallery where gilt-framed portraits lined both flanking walls. These I would have liked to have lingered and examined in detail, but my guide did not slacken her pace so I was only permitted to catch brief glimpses of men attired in all manner of costume and one or two ladies wearing nothing at all save for the occasional muff or fur stole.

Then we came to the far end of the passage and the dark lady merged into the panelled wall, leaving me to assume the room I was looking for lay behind a double walnut door fitted with a brass handle and finger plate.

I cannot be certain if I turned the handle and pushed the left door or if it opened of its own accord, but open it did and I was able to enter the room beyond.

Another room similar to the portrait gallery save that the walls were covered with well-packed book shelves and there was a table standing in the centre, complete with attendant straight-back chairs. Light came from fanlights set into the high ceiling.

On the table lay a massive book bound in blue leather. A chair was drawn back as though waiting for me to sit on it. I sat and turned back the front cover and read the black block inscription:

THE BOOK OF FORBIDDEN KNOWLEDGE
by
Buto
Translated by The Reverend Henry Cooper
from the original in 1815
Printed by Walders and Smollet
Patermasters Row, London 1817

I turned over another page and instantly wished I had brought my glasses for the print was exceedingly small, similar to that one comes across in many early Victorian novels, but so great was my interest I eased the book forward so that it received a more generous flood of light and forced my eyes to read the text.

'ASHERIAN BELOVED OF WADJET

'Asherian was born a princess of the house of Kalutina, one of many children sired by Akhenaton Prince of Amarna, who not wishing her to share the common fate of royal children after his death, dedicated her to the service of Wadjet the Serpent.

'And it is recorded that the god gazed upon Asherian and became enslaved by her beauty, so much so he gave her gifts such as have never before been granted to a mortal. And the greatest of these was the knowledge of how to reach those shadow lands that lie beyond the one we know.

'Yet there was one price that Asherian had to pay for all eternity. She must never gaze upon any being, mortal or immortal, with favour, other than Wadjet, for he was a jealous god whose love could so easily turn to hate. He spoke thus to her:

'"The earth and those lands that lie beyond the one we know, all are yours. But there is one fruit you must not pick, one garden in which you may not walk, for to do so will turn the spark of my never-sleeping anger into an all-consuming flame, and you from being the most exalted of mortal women will become the Cursed. The being from which all men will shrink and you will wander the time lanes for all eternity, scorned, feared. . ."

'And for many decades Asherian heeded the words of her god-lover and behold she was great in the land of Egypt and in all lands that lie beyond the one we know, but there came a time when the eternal youth and beauty that was hers demanded the joy that can only come from the homage paid by one of her own kind and she began to long to lay upon the bed of mortal lust, take to herself a son of earth.

'Now there lived at that time in the city of Thebes a widow of moderate wealth whose most guarded treasure was her son Armenda; a youth of great beauty and pious mien, an object of much heart-break to any maiden who had gazed upon his face. But his mother had determined that he should enter the service of the god Anubis so that she would have one waiting to guide her to the land of the dead when her time came.

'And Asherian saw the youth in the market place and so lusted after him her soul knew no peace by night or day. And he, looking down from his bedroom window, gazed upon her unveiled face, her beauty enhanced by moonlight, and, behold, two flames intermingled and from that time onward each was damned in the sight of god and man.

'Yet it is recorded for a brief spell they knew great joy for Asherian who had lain in the love bed of an immortal god, knew the secret of a thousand and one ways of unendurable pleasure, so that there came the day Armenda prayed to his beloved, saying:

'"Now let me die for having reached the peak of ecstasy, life no longer has a goal for me to aim for and I would sleep in the arms of true death."

'And Asherian, knowing that the god Wadjet must know she had fallen and would most surely strike when it so pleased him to do so, and wishing to spare her mortal lover the torments that would soon be visited upon her, summoned Madket, handmaiden to Anubis, god of the dead, and implored her:

'"Guide my beloved through the underworld and shield him from the rage of Wadjet, leaving me to bear the punishment intended for two."

'And Madket placed the soul of Armenda in an earthenware

jar and carried it through the underworld and presently broke it on the banks of the red river. And Armenda slept the endless dream sleep and from then on knew neither joy or despair.

'Asherian did not have to wait long for one night Wadjet appeared to her in his most terrible form, a great flesh-coloured snake who reared up against the sky and with a roaring voice that made the earth tremble said:

'"I loved you above all beings, mortal or immortal, and I have given you gifts beyond price and all lands that lie beyond the one we know were yours in which you might besport yourself and next to the immortal gods, you were the most worshipped being.

'"But now must my anger be appeased or it will feed upon itself and destroy the land we know, so listen to my irrevocable will.

'"I take from you the gift of eternal youth, but never will you be seared by the cold hand of old age.

'"I hereby take from you your beauty, but you will never be cursed by ugliness.

'"You will walk the earth until the sun grows cold, but never know illness or be struck down by disease.

'"I do now set upon you my mark and thus will man and god know I have cursed you for all eternity. I take from you your hair and in itself will grow miniature likenesses of myself and their venom will destroy those who have not been driven mad when they gaze upon that which you cannot hide forever."

'The great snake-god shrank in size and presently appeared as a slim young man with an elongated head. His skin was as white as a slab of snow in moonlight, his large slanting eyes pools that reflected the purple twilight of melancholy. His voice now deep with vibrant undertones.

'"Yet it is forbidden that even I condemn anyone to a limitless future that is not lit, no matter how faintly, by the lamp of hope. So listen well to what I am about to say and may my words give you strength to endure the torment which will be yours in the centuries to come.

'"When you meet a mortal man whose love enables him to pass through the underworld, then cross the red river, and is able to see the beauty which is only hidden under tired skin and pouched eyes, who has the courage to clasp your naked head to his breast, then will the curse be lifted, all gifts restored and the madness of happiness be yours."

'The god then became a slim shadow that glided away and was seen no more and Princess Asherian released a terrible cry and flung herself upon the ground, pleaded with the Light Lords that this curse not be visited upon her, but when she rose her glorious red hair lay upon the desert sand and her head covered with boil-like protuberances that presently erupted and released small likenesses of the Snake God, and they roared with tiny gaping jaws.

'Many are the stories told of the Princess Asherian from that day on, but the most enthralling is that which relates how a companion was sent to relieve her loneliness, on the long road to eternity.

'A woman, dark, lean and unlovely, with black deep sunken eyes and the princess recognized her as Madket who had carried Armenda's soul through the underworld and who had also been cursed by Wadjet. And she said to the princess:

' "I must walk in your shadow until you are freed by one who has conquered fear."

'The princess permitted herself a pale smile even while the evil crop stirred on her hairless head. "So there is a vein of mercy in the god's anger. But I think we must abandon our ancient names and take on those more fitting to our new status. I will call myself the non-royal Princess Helena. And you, Madket, onetime hand-maiden to the gods, how will you be called?'

' "If it pleases Madame the Princess I will be called Gredelsa, now battle-maiden to she who was once the beloved of Wadjet."

'And so it was that these two accursed immortals wandered the earth looking for one who would set the princess free and although many were chosen none remained once they had looked upon her naked head. Then the Princess Helena appealed to the gods for permission to visit those lands which lay beyond the one we know, but her plea was refused. Instead she was granted sway over the limbo that does not exist in the empty place between yesterday and tomorrow; here she could create forms and beings that amused and sometimes instructed for all mental creation is based on long ago acquired knowledge.

'And the princess from the richness of her mind created a realm called Far Acres, then together with the battle-maiden Gredelsa, built a house and people it with those elementals that will take on any shape that was required and perform those simple duties that might be expected from mortal servants.'

*

I slammed the book shut and gazed around the library, taking notice of the packed shelves of beautifully bound books that gave the impression they were often dusted but rarely opened.

I took one red leather-bound volume from its place between green ones of gigantic proportions and read the gilt-etched title.

WAR IN HEAVEN
by
Conrad von Holstein

This was repeated in large black lettering on the title page with the following information: *An account of the mighty conflict and its effect on the Land we know and those lands which lie beyond.*

But when I turned over the ensuing pages of which there must have been two hundred and fifty or more, all were blank. The same was true of the flanking green volumes entitled:

UNNATURAL ENMITIES AND THEIR DISPOSAL
by
Conrad von Holstein

and:

INTO THE VORTEX
by
Erich von Holstein

I had no doubt such would have been so of any book I care to lay hand to; the princess and her companion favoured the trappings of literature but not its essence. Save for the book which lay upon the table, *The Book of Forbidden Knowledge*, which contained that interesting account of the princess's origins. But of course one's own biography must be of burning interest no matter how inaccurate it might be; and I could not decide if all this jargon of Ancient Egyptian gods was intended to be accepted as unvarnished fact or some kind of allegorical fiction, based very loosely on fact.

I replaced all three books, left *The Book of Forbidden Knowledge* upon on the table, and vacated the library by another door set in the end wall, only to emerge into another long room which was the most bizarre of any I had yet seen.

The walls were covered with thick blue curtains which hung in graceful and clearly carefully arranged drapes; a fitted carpet of a much deeper hue seemed to cling to my feet as I went forward, while on both sides stood little white round tables with gilt legs that perfectly matched the attendant chairs.

Seated at these tables were ladies and gentlemen (the definition seemed to be apt at that time) attired in early eighteenth century costume. Blue satin coats, high-heeled shoes; all complete with patches and paint, quizzing glasses, beringed fingers, diamond bedecked necks, the occasional glittering order on noble breast.

But no one in this colourful assembly spoke or moved. I walked the length of the room and back, then half of its length again, for a little silver plaque standing on one table atttracted my attention. On it was etched in black lettering.

CONVERSATION ROOM

I looked around at the motionless assembly and had to admit they did give the impression they were all engaged in conversation – of rather frivolous nature, for many faces wore inane grins or smiles, and some hands were raised as though emphasizing a point, and I did think it might be interesting to know what they all were saying.

I walked to the tall windows and raised one heavy blue curtain and tried to see what lay outside, but darkness was complete with not so much as a hint of moon or stars. In fact there could well be nothing of substance out there, exactly as when I had peered through the bungalow window – in reverse.

I went back to the table on which stood the silver plaque and suddenly realised that it partly hid a silver arrow set in the table itself. I looked in the direction the arrow pointed and saw a small white button surrounded by a handsome brass ring inserted in the wall beside an Adam fireplace. Under it was yet another plaque on which was inscribed:

PRESS FOR CONVERSATION

I went over to the fireplace and gazed down on this invitation for some little while having long ago come to the conclusion Far Acres had more than a touch of Alice-in-Wonderlandness and I would not have been all that surprised if pressing the button resulted in me growing so fast my head hit the ceiling.

Instead when I did press the button, I experienced something of an anticlimax when nothing happened at all. Not at once. But then a head jerked round, a hand was lowered, a murmur came from the far end of the room, then the rumble of more than one masculine voice, until I was looking upon talking, gesturing, very look-alive people.

I walked along the line of tables and finally sat upon a vacant chair and found myself facing two middle-aged gentlemen: one with a florid red face and attired in a silver-coloured coat and flowing lace cravat; the other much younger and attired in white satin. The elder addressed me with a pompous tone of voice:

'I have just been maintaining, sir, that it invariably rains in wet weather, but this young jackanapes will have none of it. Talks of water coming up from the ground. Can't understand the demned water wouldn't have been in the ground if it hadn't rained in the first place.'

The young man yawned and raised his quizzing glass and stared at a young girl seated at the next table whose naked shoulders rose up from her low cut amber-coloured dress. Although she sat with her back to us I noticed the flaming red hair with an unaccountable quickening of my heart beat. Presently the young man yawned again and said with every sign of complete boredom:

'Finest pair of feminine shoulders I've seen in a month of wet Sundays, sink me if they aren't. But rain you say? In wet weather? Not always. Demnable fog wet. No rain. Blasted dew comes out of the pesky air. Something to do with the temperature, don't you know?'

The red-faced man grunted. 'Next thing you'll say is the sun never shines when it's dark.'

The young man wagged an elegant forefinger. 'But it does. Not necessarily where it's dark, but the demnable thing is shining somewhere.'

The red-faced man addressed me. 'What's your opinion, sir?'
I spoke carelessly. 'I think you two gentlemen would make excellent politicians. You speak much but say nothing.'

The young man looked at me through his quizzing glass. 'Bit strong there, sir. Demn me if it wasn't. Could be the beginning of an insult, sink me if there isn't.'

I was about to murmur an apology for I am that kind of person who really believes in peace at any price, when a soft lilting voice came from my left.

'Don't take any notice of those two. Or anyone else in this madhouse.'

I jerked my head to the left and saw the girl with the red hair and bare shoulders had also turned round to reveal herself as Katrina. I gazed upon her with a blend of pleasure and alarm.

'Hallo! I've been told I mustn't talk to you.'

She nodded and swung round to face me completely. 'Don't take the slightest notice of that. The princess still thinks she's the bed-mate of a god and can order people around as it pleases her. I intend to see you anytime I wish and you must want to see me.'

I instantly nodded most vigorously. 'I do. Indeed I do.'

'Then ignore the old sausage. Tell her to get the snakes off her head before she starts shouting the odds. Really, she makes me sick.'

I raised my hand and motioned to the two conversationalists. 'What's this all about?' They're talking awful rubbish.'

'Oh, this is just an example of the princess playing with herself. If you get what I mean. Believe it or not, but this lot are really bits of herself. And she's decked them out as belonging to the period of history she enjoyed most. Mad isn't it?'

'Most enthralling,' I corrected. 'Everyone looks so real.'

Katrina giggled – a most enchanting sound. 'But they are – at this very moment. When you pushed the button you did something to your own brain which had the effect of making you see what old snake-head wants you to see – and hear. But you mustn't ask any more questions or you'll make it even more complicated than it already is.'

A light tap on my shoulder resulted in me turning my head, and I stared into the young man's eyes, becoming unreasonably angry when seeing his mocking smile. His voice drawled in the best Sir Percy Blakeney manner.

'My dear fellow, aren't you going to introduce the lady, demn me!'

I had no other recourse but to rise and introduce the young girl whom I scarcely knew myself.

'This is. . .'

I paused and she too rose and performed a charming little bow.

'Countess Katrina de Monford. At your service, gentlemen.'

The florid man in the silver-coloured coat muttered: 'Are you, be gad!' and somehow shuffled to his feet, then added: 'Sir Godfrey Makepiece, if it so pleases you, ma'am,' while the young man in white bowed deeply and said: 'Lord Tony Palmer, your devoted slave, my lady.' Then with an audacity that enraged me: 'Allow me to make room for you at this table. There's room particularly if our unknown friend will be so kind as to draw back a trifle.'

To my disgust Katrina accepted this insolent invitation and was soon seated between the two men, which at least allowed me to watch the changing expressions in her eyes and the enchanting smile that played around her mouth. When we were all seated Lord Palmer – he in the white coat – looked at me with something close to a sneer (what a difference the presence of a pretty girl will make to the conduct of some men) and asked:

'Since we have all introduced ourselves, what about you giving yourself a name, sir.' Instantly Katrina raised a protesting hand and spoke loudly:

'No please. You must not know his name. He is simply referred to as Chu-Chu.'

For a moment the two men reverted back to being wax models, expressions of horrified astonishment froze on their faces, then they exploded back into a facsimile of life, the alternating expressions flickering like faulty electric bulbs. Lord Tony was the first to speak.

'Spoken out of turn there, demn it. Bad habit. Great honour to have met Chu-Chu.'

Sir Godfrey cleared his throat and gave every impression of being a man who is struggling in the morass of acute embarrassment.

'May I reciprocate my friend's sentiments. Couldn't agree more. Can see at a glance that you're a past master of the art of polite conversation.'

'Keen observer,' Lord Tony added. 'Eye like a hawk, mind of an eagle.'

Lord Tony stifled another yawn. 'Took the demned words out of me blasted mouth. Sink me if you didn't.'

Katrina gave me a conspiratorial wink, then asked in a mock serious voice:

'Is it not a fact that we never have hot weather when it freezes?'

Lord Tony raised his quizzing glass and again directed his gaze at her naked shoulders. 'Demned penetrating question. Proves she's not just a pair of pretty shoulders.'

Sir Godfrey nodded slowly and gave the impression he was on the verge of dropping off to sleep. 'Correction is as correction goes. But I defy her to face up to the three letter word Why. Or is it why? That'll floor her. Always does.'

Katrina gave me another wink. 'Stephen, darling impossible Stephen. Our secret name. Please don't look like that. I'm only trying to make conversation – polite conversation, which is like all other conversation only no one is rude if they can help it – and not a word makes sense.'

'But there must be a point to it,' I murmured. 'I mean these people – things are toys of the gods. And when gods speak, even indirectly, what they say means something – most of it nasty.'

'Stephen darling, now you're talking. . .'

'Commonsense which is not all that common seeing there's very little of it about.'

'But, Stephen, the thin red line of rationality runs through a tortuous plain and the poor little ego can soon be lost. You do follow me?'

I shook my head. 'Not really.'

'You're not all that bright. Listen. The shortest distance between two points is a straight line; a point has no width, depth, or circumference, so it does not exist, therefore a straight line cannot exist. . . Oh, Stephen, just think what that adds up to. Life is an illusion set in an unlimited sea of nothing.'

I clasped hands to shaking head and tried to bring peace to a seething brain. My cry went out across the plain of space-time:

'Please stop. The veil of ignorance was the kindest gift given to man; don't tear it aside.'

'That's what I've been trying to tell you. Listen to me and you won't go far right.'

'There you go again.'

'Left is the twisting path that leads to the underworld. And it is decreed that. . .'

Sir Godfrey coughed loudly, and screwed his mouth up into a semblance of an enquiring smile.

'Sorry, beautiful shoulders, and you Lord Chu-Chu, but we are getting the impression that the young lady and yourself are venturing beyond the line which defines polite conversation. To be almost brutal, we must at least hint she is toying with the possibility of relating some very unpalatable facts.'

I took a deep breath then released a flow of words which more or less expressed my true sentiments.

'I'd rather be given some facts no matter how unpalatable, than flounder around in a bog of conjecture, mythology and unanswerable questions. For example. . .'

Every head jerked in my direction, every mouth opened and the princess's voice spoke from every tongue:

'Chu-Chu, leave the conversation room at once. Report to me in the morning room.'

I looked for Katrina in vain, she had disappeared. All the conversationalists again spoke in unison.

'Hurry, Chu-Chu. I am almost kept waiting.'

I left that room where motionless figures sat waiting for a button to be pressed so that they again could indulge in polite conversation – or very meaningful conversation if one could only get the hang of it – and walked quickly through the portrait gallery and out into a maze of corridors, there to follow the unhappy shade of the dark lady who glided in front of me until we reached a certain door where she promptly disappeared.

Madame the Princess was lying on her day bed still wearing a long white dress while her head was now covered by a scarlet shawl. As usual she patted a place beside her on the bed and waited until I was comfortably seated before speaking.

'Well, Chu-Chu, do you now know more about me than you did?'

'I might do.'

'Perhaps you'll explain exactly what you mean by that.'

'If it wasn't for the . . . the. . .'

'The snakes on my head. Don't be afraid to mention them. I know they're there.'

'Very well, if it wasn't for the snakes on your head I would have dismissed everything I've seen, heard or read about as so much moonshine. And even now I can't go along with you being the ex-girlfriend of an Egyptian god.'

She traced a pattern on the bedspread with her forefinger and for a while did not speak, and I was forced to wonder what fantastic explanation she was dreaming up for my benefit. Then she took my hand and said quietly:

'The gods do not belong to any particular country, or, for that matter, world. 'Chu-Chu, do you really believe that a species of monkey evolved into a creature capable of creating a machine civilization in the short period of one hundred thousand years, did so unaided? A race of super beings were programmed into that great ball of life that exploded long, long ago. We have talked of this matter before but as yet you lack the ability to believe this fundamental truth. Wadjet is one of the oldest of these gods – superbeings – who is identified with a snake. The reptiles were at one time chosen to put up a candidate for the sovereignty of intelligent life on this planet. Chu-Chu, never for one moment doubt the existence of the immortal gods.'

'We're talking too much.'

'Talk is the basis of action. That is why I invented the polite conversation gallery.'

'I was there. . .'

Her hand suddenly squeezed mine with such strength I cried out; the princess's voice was no less harsh.

'And you were talking to a creature I told you to ignore. And I'll swear by all the gods she was about to tell you that you are not yet fitted to know.'

'But she was there – among those animated dummies – and she spoke to me first. The only real one. I just couldn't ignore her.'

The silk shawl heaved slightly, at a point just over the crown of her head; the princess patted it and the bulge subsided. 'Don't think for one moment I do not know what pretty little dream is drifting around in your mind. The sweet little girl who should have lived next door, but alas never did. Don't go mooning after her. I will not have it. I will not have it. Do you hear me?'

Hysterical women were part of my profession and I had become an expert in dealing with them, but the princess was no ordinary woman and I just couldn't understand her apparent fear of Katrina, there being so far as I could determine no other reason for this irrational behaviour.

I said: 'I am not chasing this child and have only found her to be amusing. But if we should meet sometime in the future I cannot promise not to talk to her. But she is much too young and inexperienced for my taste, so your fears are completely without foundation.'

Now she assumed a coy demeanour and swayed from side to side, an affectation I found to be revolting. There was even the suggestion of a simper in her voice when she spoke:

'Then you are not drawn to youth? You consider maturity appealing? How remarkable!'

This was so out of character I gazed upon her with amazement, even though a growing attachment still drew me to her. I made what was not perhaps a diplomatic reply:

'An impossibility would be the ideal – youth plus experience. But alas one cannot hope to find that residing in one body.'

Now she sent out wave after wave of bubbling laughter and it seemed as if I had been permitted a glimpse of an irresponsible child who would torment any adult who lacked the ability of keeping her under control. Eventually I took a step forward and raised my hand.

'Stop this instant or I'll slap you into obedience.'

The laughter was turned off with the abruptness of a pulled switch and was replaced by a sudden spurt of anger.

'You would dare to strike me, Chu-Chu? A little pouf dare to raise his hand to a princess of an ancient line.'

'For your own good,' I retorted boldly. 'Your hysteria was getting out of hand.'

'Out of hand? You walk on ground, Chu-Chu, that might well crumble beneath your feet. But you are becoming interesting. Would you beat me – for my good? Such is always the excuse the strong use when they beat the weak. Yet did you not know the strong can sometimes derive pleasure from submitting to the tyranny of the weak? There are many colourful by-ways into which the soul can wander in its search for bizarre experience and should we not all drink from many cups before facing eternity?'

'You are playing with ideas,' I said.

'Am I? Yet I am not a playful creature as a rule. Know you I am a chained tigress who could tear your arm from its socket as easily as you would pluck a weed from the ground. Believe me when I say I have struck a man blind for smiling at a maid and ignited a fire in the brain of a woman who would seek out and tell the world my secret.'

I drew back and would have freed my arm from her grip but she would not release me. But I still possessed the courage to speak the truth as I saw it, for instinct told me that if I let this woman – or whatever she might be – manacle me with the chains of fear, I would be lost.

'If you tell the truth then you must be a monster.'

'Of course I am a monster, Chu-Chu. What else can a creature be who has snakes for hair? And if I am a monster then I have every right to behave like one. But . . . but do not force me to dwell on horrible possibilities. I would rather talk of you having a body to play with that housed both youth and experience, plus a soul willing to love, honour and obey. Like Katrina no doubt. Sweet, loving, merry, teasing, young, obedient Katrina.'

I expected another hysterical outburst, but she continued to speak quite rationally.

'Have patience, Chu-Chu. Have patience. When the curse is lifted and it must be quite soon. I know . . . know . . . it must be quite soon. And what will happen afterwards I have no way of knowing.'

I nodded as though in agreement and this seemed to make her happy, for she smiled then pressed my hand. 'I would rest for a while, Chu-Chu, if they will let me. Dream perhaps of those days which may yet come again. Now run away and play, but don't go back to the polite conversation gallery – you won't be able to find your way back. But you may go back to the library. Yes, I don't mind your reading modern drama. It's called – oh dear my mind is going – *Medusa Reborn* – all silly and dramatic, but quite interesting in parts. Written by Eric Maultravers. A lovely boy.' She sighed deeply. 'I had to light a fire in his brain eventually. He was not satisfied with merely writing, he wanted to publish.'

'What –?' I began, but she quickly interrupted.

'Please don't ask me what happened to him. Go away and read some if not all of the manuscript. Some of your questions may well be answered. Come back when I have the time to teach you how to play with the stars.'

I found myself tip-toeing from the room for she fell asleep instantly, but I did not allow my gaze to dwell upon her face for asleep she looked strangely young.

I found my way back to the library quite easily and was not all that surprised to find that now there was no door at the far end and a different book lay open upon the table. It was so quiet in the room I could not even hear myself walking, suggesting that the sense of hearing had been taken from me, if indeed I had ever possessed it. I made a slow tour of the four walls, took out several well bound blank leaved books, tried once again to unsuccessfully peer through windows, then walked to the table and sat down.

The book was a typed manuscript bound by means of metal clips and cardboard covers. Someone had inscribed the title with a black felt pen.

MEDUSA REBORN
by
Eric Maultravers

I turned the title page and slowly read the author's introduction. It riveted my attention even though I doubted if I would have the courage to peruse the manuscript from cover to cover. I too was a writer and everything was grist that came to my mill. Suppose I too surrendered to the urge to commit all I had learned about Madame the Princess to paper? I could never write other than for publication and so would sooner or later merit having a fire lit in my brain. If I did not go mad of my own accord long before I decided to put fingers to typewriter.

II

Medusa Reborn

Authors' Note

This is a brief account of my meeting with that creature who styles herself Madame the Princess Helena Landi. Should anyone read this manuscript, to them I would say, seek her out and destroy her, together with the minion that is her shadow – Gredelsa, or, as I think she should be called, Griseldis, the battlemaiden.

I am not all that certain if either of them can be destroyed, for the princess has power that is derived from the very life force from which the universe was formed. At least that is my opinion, but I could quite well be on the verge of madness. But having seen what is hidden under wig or shawl I can have no doubt she belongs to another species than my own or any creature that walks, crawls, flies or swims on this planet today.

I pray to whatever god that hears me that my sanity will be spared long enough for me to complete this account and it may fall into the hands of someone who will believe and have the power to act before it is too late.

Eric Maultravers

*

CHAPTER ONE

It was at a party to celebrate my engagement to Fiona that I first heard of the Princess Helena Landi. We had taken two rooms at the small, but very popular hotel The White Hart at Mumford, this being situated at the end of the great motor road that leads direct to London.

We were very much in love. Yes, I know that's giggle-making these days and I should have said we fancied each other or we turned each other on, but I can honestly say the electricity that ran between us was very much more than mere physical attraction and if fate had dealt us a better hand we would have been partners for life.

We were not only lovers but very good friends and that I believe to be the only good basis for a perfect marriage.

I was twenty-eight, Fiona twenty-four, and for two years we told each other that marriage would spoil our relationship. Then came the need for a symbolic fusion of bodies and souls, the result I suppose of generations of respectable forbears who looked upon 'living in sin' as the number one crime after murder – or even before it.

The first stage on the road to matrimony is engagement, which provided a good excuse for me to buy Fiona a diamond ring that made all her girl friends grind their teeth with envy and throw a party where everyone got nicely, even politely semi-drunk.

Let me say here and now both Fiona and I were well-heeled having been born to the right parents, who had wisely decided to give us lucrative shares in the respective family businesses, then get divorced and leave us much to our own devices. A fair example of upper-middle class family life, but one we were determined not to emulate.

Around nine o'clock most of us were pleasantly woozy and those not staying at the hotel were talking of hiring cars to take them home come midnight, when Reggie Masters who was bedding down Margie Broadfield and had booked in the night before, said:

'We've got ourselves a real live princess in this 'ere hotel.'

This item of information registered after a while and even generated a spark of interest. Someone asked:

'Go on! One of ours?'

'No. According to the chambermaid who does her as well as us, she's the Princess Helena Landi and no one has seen her without a bloody great wig or a scarf thing.'

Charlie Wentworth lurched backwards then rolled his eyes. 'Maybe she suffers from dandruff or falling hair.'

But Fiona who was always looking for someone to feel sorry for, shook her dark head in gentle reproof. 'Poor lady. I'm sure there must be a sad reason why she keeps her head covered and I for one hope it's not catching.'

Charlie sat down. 'That's a thought! I'm giving all ladies who wear wigs a wide berth from now on. I'd hate to lose my crowning glory.'

Reggie dropped his second bomb.

'Moreover this pate-covered princess has a gruesome attendant who spat at Margie this morning.'

There was a storm of disbelieving growls until Margie herself with much wide-eyes grimacing and violent nodding, ventured to give a supporting account.

'True. Honestly. I met her coming down the stairs, where they curve and I sort of accidentally like bumped into her and she spat at me. Well, she made a spitting noise. I've never been so frightened. Well you don't expect to meet spitting women in the White Hart.'

'Only the Ritz Carlton,' I suggested and was rather hurt when this smart remark was not even greeted by a single laugh.

'I can't remember who suggested the mad idea, but I was dead against it from the start.

'Look,' I shouted over the din which had broken out, 'the poor woman is entitled to her privacy. God knows they charge enough for it in this place.'

'But we only want to borrow a cup of sugar,' Reggie protested and I could see he was becoming more than politely slightly drunk. 'One of us knocks on the door and presents an empty cup and asks for a refill of sugar. If the dragon appears we'll all make spitting noises, if it's the princess it's curtsies all round.'

Morris Browning, who is all of six foot three, gave us his loud agreement. 'Very civilized behaviour. I always bob in the presence of royalty; not that I've moved in such exalted circles lately.'

Fiona clung to my arm and begged me to at least try to stop them, but to be honest I had drunk as much and perhaps more than was good for me, so instead of restraining this stupid escapade, I found myself, together with Fiona, leading it.

We ignored the lift and went trooping up the stairs, those who stumbled were helped by the more sure-footed, until the first floor corridor with its row of bright-blue doors each flaunting a little brass number stretched out on either side.

'It's number seven,' Margie stated. 'The chambermaid said number seven.'

All the doors looked impressive (for hotel doors) and number seven was no exception, except it was further enhanced by a small plaque that had been fastened to the central frame on which was painted a gilt cobra with its hood expanded. Under this in black lettering was the inscription:

HEH THE PRINCESS HELENA LANDI

There was a fair amount of giggling and arguing as to who should present the cup, until finally a tall girl with short blonde hair said she would brave the tigresses in their den and grabbing the cup went boldly up to the door and tapped on the panels.

An eerie silence descended upon our group and I think that most of us began to realise that we were being very silly and if someone actually parted with a cup of sugar and then told us to push off, there would be nothing more than an anti-climax.

The door was opened so fast it seemed as if the portal had disappeared while closed, then re-emerged fully open, together with a tall lean and grim figure attired in a black dress.

Never have I seen before or since a more disagreeable-looking woman. A long thin death-white face, black to greyish hair that was wound round the head several times and kept in place by large tortoiseshell combs. The eyes were black and deep set, the lips so thin as to be almost non-existent. Her hands, which were never still, were long and claw-like.

She glared at us and I can remember thinking that woman though she be, I still wouldn't like to turn my back on her on a dark night. She radiated a kind of ferocious power that seemed to manifest when she barked one word:

'Yes?'

The tall blonde girl who was called Billie, presented her tea cup and said hurriedly: 'Please can we have some sugar?'

One hand moved with the speed of a cobra and struck the cup from the girl's hand and I for one watched it go bouncing over the floor to break against the far wall, with startled astonishment. Reggie was the first to speak.

'Look here, there was no need to do that.'

The hand came out again and made a derisive gesture, while the harsh voice spat out another word.

'Away.'

'It would seem that we are not welcome,' Reggie informed us. 'Moreover we must depart sugarless.'

Fiona, who had been against this senseless charade from the beginning, pushed her way forward and addressed the irate woman.

'I'm sorry, we shouldn't have bothered you and I apologize for myself and our party.' She turned and gestured all of us back to the stairs. 'Come let's go. A cup of black coffee all round would not be out of place.'

We were halfway to the stairs when a sweet feminine voice that spoke flawless English enhanced by a slight mid-European accent made us pause.

'Gredelsa, let the young people come in.'

The woman looked back over one shoulder, irritation expressed in every line of her face.

'But, Madame the Princess –'

'Do as I say. Invite them into our drawing-room. I will receive them.'

We all exchanged glances, shoulders were at least mentally shrugged, then we all turned about and entered the room, being careful not to brush against the woman called Gredelsa as we did so.

The drawing room was what one might expect to find in an

expensive motorway hotel; a few small armchairs scattered around an adjustable table, a cocktail cabinet, large television set and an artificial coal gas fire. No one dared to sit down until the princess entered the room and lowered herself into the most comfortable armchair. That peerless voice spoke again.

'Those of you who can sit down on the chairs, the others make themselves as comfortable as possible on the floor.'

There followed a shuffling, bumping and self-conscious grinning period which finally terminated by most of us sitting on the floor.

The princess addressed her attendant. 'Gredelsa, where are your manners? Refreshments for our guests.'

As 'refreshments' were the reason for our being there I thought it best to politely refuse, but had scarcely opened my mouth than our hostess smiled and shook her head.

'A glass of white wine will do no harm and will enable me to dispense hospitality. Gredelsa, see to it.'

The woman departed – with a stiff back and tilted chin – and I began to examine her mistress – not a term I would use normally but one that seemed to suit the princess – and decided she must be a woman in her late forties who looked younger in the artificial light. A pale oval face that retained a vestige of a former beauty. The eyes were dark, large and most certainly enchanting. They reflected intelligence, an ageless spirit and the strange ability to change colour – or such was my impression – with her prevailing mood.

Now she was gazing upon this crowd of young people with kindly intent her eyes were a deep sombre brown, but when Gredelsa delayed in returning with the glasses of white wine, they turned to blazing amber such as might have marked the presence of an angry tigress.

'Gredelsa, we are being kept waiting.'

The monstrous red wig was out of keeping with the elegant black dress relieved by white lace at the neck and wrists and I found myself wondering why she wore it and could only decide that she must have lost her own hair through sickness although she still had thick eyebrows of a rich reddish colour. Her face had been skilfully made up, but even so had not entirely eradicated the lines that either suffering or time had etched around eyes and mouth.

Then her attention was directed at Fiona and the eyes changed again.

They took on the unblinking intensity of a snake. I saw her right hand open and close, the pink tongue that darted out and licked full lips, then was as quickly withdrawn. From that time onward I was both fascinated and frightened by Princess Helena Landi.

Yet she entertained us with a light subtle wit that completely captivated our party – including Fiona. I think at first there was a certain restraint, the wig coming in for a fair amount of whispered ribald remarks, but after a while everyone succumbed to the woman's undoubted charm.

She gave us all an enquiring glance.

'You have been entertaining? For some reason?'

Reggie who always liked to hear the sound of his own voice, seemed to have elected himself as our spokesman.

'Eric and Fiona have decided to become engaged.'

'And that is a matter of celebration?'

Reggie cast a quick glance around the room, then said with a smirk:

'That's a matter of opinion. But it's the event engagement leads up to that's real dodgy. The white funeral.'

'The white funeral? I have not heard of this before. Do people die after becoming engaged?'

A roar of laughter greeted this question (as afterwards I became convinced she intended) and this encouraged Reggie to play to the gallery.

'Sure thing, your highness. There's no life after marriage.'

She had switched her gaze from Fiona to the room in general, but I could still detect the unblinking snake-like aspect of her eyes. Her voice had a vibrant tone when she spoke.

'My title is not a royal one. I am addressed either as Princess or Madame. To servants and menials I can be styled Highness.'

This announcement rather damped the atmosphere until the princess smiled and ordered more wine.

'I think my leg is being pulled – that is still the correct term is it not? You are making fun at me. No one dies when couple get married. Of course not. That custom belongs to another time –

another place. You must forgive any errors I make but I have not long been in your country.'

'Yet you speak excellent English, Madame,' I commented.

Her unblinking stare was directed to me and involuntarily I shuddered. 'Ah! The male half of the engagement! Yes, I speak all languages fluently, including several eastern dialects. But this is not surprising as I have had a long time in which to perfect them.'

'And your maid?' I enquired driven by some impish urge to pester her with questions. 'Is she equally gifted?'

The eyes now sparkled with amusement and I had the most eerie feeling that she had in some way entered my mind and could watch each thought as it was formed.

'My maid! Yes, I suppose she is my handmaiden among other roles. And yes, I'd say she is equally gifted. Perhaps more so. And she has walked the earth for a very long time. Much longer than myself. But let us to more mundane matters. This party of naughty children amuse me and perhaps I will provide them with some light entertainment.'

She looked round the room with the careless-care of a stage magician who is about to summons his stooge from the audience, then directed her gaze and pointed finger at Fiona.

'You my dear! Yes indeed – pretty dear such as I have not seen for a long while. Come to me.'

Fiona drew back and slid her hand into mine and I was about to protest when the thought flashed unbidden across my mind that there was no reason to do so; the princess was about to demonstrate some harmless trick and it would be churlish to intervene.

I pushed Fiona forward, ignoring her struggles, joining in the laughter; she ceased to struggle when the princess's hands were laid lightly on her head and allowed herself to be turned round so that she faced the audience.

I must confess to a feeling of guilt when I saw my future wife standing there with unsmiling face and frightened eyes. And that woman wearing a red wig that seemed much too high, suggesting that it might fall off at any moment; whose eyes were now glittering like a snake that has finally hypnotized a succulent young bird.

She ran her hands over Fiona's naked shoulders, then down her arms to her hands. I think she must have dug her fingernails into soft palms for the girl suddenly gasped and shook each hand, then opened her mouth to its fullest extent.

The princess raised her right arm and announced in a loud dramatic tone of voice:

'Ladies and gentlemen, you are about to witness the trick I have performed before all the crowned heads of Europe including the pearly queen of Bethnal Green.'

She laid one hand on the top of Fiona's head and the other under her chin and whispered in her ear. It gradually emerged into view. At the very back of the gaping mouth as though forcing itself up from the throat, then sliding forward until it became necessary to sidle its oval shape over the lower teeth.

A golden egg. Gleaming in the lamplight. The size of a chicken egg, it seeped over the stretched lips and fell into the princess's hand. She laid it on the table and we all watched it rock back and forth until a neat hair-line crack appeared round the centre; then the two halves parted and a pretty gold and green snake undulated across the table until Gredelsa swept it into a glass bowl. I watched the little creature form a neat coil with its diamond-shaped gold head resting on top.

Someone made a sick noise and someone else exclaimed: 'Oh, my Gawd!' and Fiona closed her mouth with an audible snap, then after a terrified glance round the room came running to me like a child to its mother.

'Take me away from her,' she pleaded. 'Please take me away from her.'

I half carried her from the room, dimly aware of Gredelsa's glare and the princess's gentle smile and did not stop until we were back in our own room, where I laid her gently on the bed.

Presently she whispered: 'Eric, never let me go near that woman again. She wants me for some reason. And she can get inside me. I could feel her, she did something to my mind. Let's go a long way off. . . So far she cannot find me.'

'We'll leave here tomorrow morning,' I promised.

'Now . . . now . . .'

Her eyes closed, her head went on to one side and so far as I could see she was fast asleep.

The remainder of our ill-fated engagement party returned

and many and varied were the explanations as to what we had
seen.

'Producing an egg from an open mouth is old hat,' Reggie
stated. 'It's what was in the egg that I object to. I mean suppose
the egg had split while it was in Fiona's mouth?'

'It was so small and wriggly,' Billie maintained. 'It could
have so easily slid down into Fiona's stomach and made a nest
there.'

This caused an uproar until I managed to quieten them all
down and advised everyone who could to leave the hotel that
night, for I was certain without knowing why that the woman
up on the next floor was capable of bringing disaster to all or
anyone of us.

Without waiting for anyone to make up their minds, I
grabbed two blankets from the bed, raced down to the foyer
when I paid the bill, quietened all protests by buying the blankets for around three times their worth, then
made up a reasonable likeness to a bed in the back seat of the
car.

When I arrived back in our room everyone had departed
save for Reggie who was watching Fiona with deep concern. He
released his breath as a vast sigh of relief when I entered the
room.

'Thank whatsit you're back. I know my car won't start, I
tried it earlier on and the others are either full up or not going in
my direction. . .'

'OK, I get the message. You want a lift. Fine. Give me a hand
downstairs with Fiona, then bung your case in the boot and
we'll be off.'

He gave Fiona another apprehensive glance. 'If you're interested your bespoke keeps making funny peculiar noises.'

I paused in my task of packing an over-night case. 'Noises?
What kind of noises?'

'Snake noises. Hissing.'

I slammed the case shut and by sitting on it managed to
press the locking studs home. I looked at Reggie. 'Right, you
ready?'

He pointed to a Tesco carrier bag. 'Let's blow.'

I carried a faintly muttering Fiona to the lift, then across the
foyer to the car which I had parked in the fore court. Reggie

carried our cases and his own carrier bag. I supposed he had made arrangements to have his car picked up, although I wasn't all that interested.

Once on the motor road I put my foot down and was soon doing an average seventy mile per hour and it wasn't until we were closing on Guildford that I slowed down to below thirty and began to wonder what the rush was all about.

Reggie peered over his shoulder and announced briefly: 'Fiona is sleeping like a baby. Say, that was a pretty sick thing, wasn't it? Produce an egg with a snake inside it from a girl's mouth. In fact anyone's mouth. I can understand Fiona being upset. Do you suppose she's suffering from some kind of shock?'

I said: 'Yep, I guess so. Get her to bed is my one aim.'

We did not speak again until I turned into the quiet square where Fiona and I lived. I then asked:

'Can you make your own way home from here? Or do you want me to put you up?'

I knew he wanted to stay but I didn't encourage him, so he shrugged. 'If you can lend me a tenner I'll ring for a mini-cab.'

I nodded. 'Can do. You carry the cases and I'll get Fiona upstairs.'

This took a bit of doing for there was no lift and I had to carry my burden up three flights of stairs, then across the sitting room (Reggie having unlocked the door) and into the spacious double bedroom. When I laid Fiona on the bed she visibly relaxed, unclenched her fists, created a charming little yawn, then became still.

I turned her gently over on to her stomach, began to unbutton her dress until I was able to part it in the centre revealing her back. She did not regard a bra as either useful or necessary.

I gave an interested Reggie a cold look.

'Right, make your telephone call, then go and wait in the hall for the cab.'

He managed to look profoundly embarrassed.

'The folding green stuff. . .'

I sighed and reaching into my breast pocket took out my wallet and extracted one ten pound note. I handed it to Reggie.

'I'll be obliged if I can have that back tomorrow.'

'Dead certain the day after.'

He reluctantly left the bedroom and I heard him dialing the telephone, then speaking in a lowered voice. I went back to disrobing Fiona.

As I had had occasion to notice many times before my intended had a most beautiful back; perfectly proportioned, smooth, white flawless skin. Well fleshed without being in the least fat. Therefore it will be readily understood that having removed all that could be removed, I spent some little while in admiring my favourite scenery.

Suddenly Fiona, who up to that moment appeared to be in a deep sleep, said distinctly: 'Stop that, Eric, it's not nice.'

For some few minutes I just stood there trying to understand what was wrong with that quite justified admonishment, before understanding hit me like a thunderbolt.

Her voice was coming from a spot some three feet away from the bed.

I asked a silly question: 'Is that you, Fiona?'

'Yes, but I seem to be standing out of my body. I can see it laid out on the bed, bare back uppermost, you drooling, all as clear as daylight. And I seem to be intact out here, for I've got arms, legs, only I'm some way off the floor. My feet are, at any rate. And I've a feeling I could go higher. And, Eric, we've got company. . . That awful Gredelsa woman is here by the door. No, don't bother to look, you won't see a thing. Her lower parts are all misty so I guess she's in a ghostie state – like me.'

Despite Fiona's instruction I looked unhappily round the room but failed to see anything out of the ordinary. Finally I asked:

'Fiona, for heavens' sake what are you doing out of your body? I mean – well – shouldn't you be dead?'

'I think we all leave our bodies when asleep, but don't remember anything when we wake up. Now that awful old woman or perhaps the princess has sort of done something peculiar to my mind so that – well – here I am.'

'Right, listen. Get back into your body at once, for it's not nice for me to look at your beautiful back and know for a fact there's no you underneath it. If I make myself clear.'

'You don't and I must ask you again – cover me up. I can't very well get back into a cold body.'

I dragged two blankets over her then stood back and waited

for some sign that the tenant had come back home. After a while I asked: 'Are you getting back in yet?'

Her voice came from the region of the ceiling. 'No. The old cow won't let me. She's hovering over it and glaring at me like nobody's business.'

'Ignore her. I can't stand here guarding a breathing corpse much longer. Now. . .'

'Eric . . . I can't . . . I think . . . in fact I'm certain she's going to get in herself.'

I thrust the implication from me and shouted: 'Don't be so bloody stupid. Get back into your body this instant or I'll tan your backside so hard you won't want to get into it for a fortnight.'

'That's not much encouragement . . . and Eric believe me . . . the old cow is dissolving and going through the eyes, nose, mouth . . . sort of pouring herself in . . . please do something . . . she's in my body. . .'

Her voice faded and then ceased altogether.

But her body was showing signs of returning consciousness and I felt a blood chilling shudder run down my spine when Fiona sat up and said in a voice that was most certainly not hers:

'My mistress says if you want to get vehicle home quickly, put your own driver behind wheel.'

I knew what had happened, but I just couldn't believe it. When you've lived an ordinary life for twenty-eight years, possession by an evil entity takes quite a bit of swallowing; so for that matter does the disembodied voice of your girl friend telling you an old woman is sliding into her body. But the kind of shock treatment I had been subjected to over the past few hours is a good way of being made to adjust one's line of thinking.

'Fiona' began to dress, that is to say put on the few items of underwear she thought necessary in cold weather, then made the hell of a business in getting into a tight dress, and when – purely out of force of habit – I tried to help, something akin to a snarl was my only thanks.

She found an outdoor coat in the wardrobe, then having slipped into it, made for the door. I was soon in front asking leading questions.

'Where are you going?'

A cold stare that did not belong to Fiona's eyes. The voice was all wrong too. 'To my mistress's country estate.'

'Can I come too?'

A shrug: 'The poor little ego who cannot get back into this body will be most unhappy if you don't. Also the princess may have a use for you. Follow me.'

There are periods in all our lives when we appear to jump from one 'aware moment' to another, not realising the number of 'non-aware' moments that have been passed over.

From the very moment that I followed Fiona's body out of the main door and without being told climbed into the back of a gleaming Rolls-Royce, I have no distinct memory of anything until I stepped down on to a gravelled drive that lay before a large house. Fiona's face was turned towards me, her eyes smiled, so did her lips – then she kissed me and whispered: 'I'm back home again. The old cow vacated the very moment we left some nasty black mist, but I thought it best to sit back and behave myself.'

I all but wept with relief although so far as I could know something far worse than possession could be waiting for us in the house.

And what a strange house it was. A suggestion of a massive collection of triangles, originating no doubt from several gabled roofs, but even the deep-set windows appeared to be made up of three or more triangles when given a cursory glance. The same could be said of the large doors that were guarded by a deep porch – that in turn had a gabled roof.

Footmen wearing black velvet jackets, grey satin shirts and bright red knee-breeches, ran down the steps and removed a number of red cases, the existence of which I had not noticed before, that later proved to contain the best part of our clothes, packed and removed from our flat – when and how I had not the slightest idea.

The house interior? It is so difficult to describe. A blending of colours, thoughts, imagination, the dream-pattern of something – someone – who-slept-and-must-never-awake. Wooden stairs supported by black marble balusters, walls covered by orange black-streaked wallpaper, all dimly lit by windows with small black and white panes. Fiona clung to me when we mounted the stairs and I became aware of a dank cold draught when we came out on to the landing; a real shiver-maker such as one might expect to come from an old family vault when the rusty iron door is opened for the first time in a very long while.

The room into which we were conducted was comfortable and neatly furnished by a double divan, bleached-walnut wardrobes and tallboys and several armchairs. A grey tabby cat that had been sleeping on the bed, got up and ambled out of the door.

'I wonder where we are?' I said and Fiona answered without hesitation:

'Far Acres, the home of Madame the Princess Helena.'

That I should have known, together with other dark knowledge that lurks in the furthermost regions of the human mind; but reluctance to look upon the often ugly face of truth did not encourage revelation.

We adopted a kind of make-believe outlook. Pretended this was a country house to which we had been invited for the week-end and if strange and rather kinky things happened to either of us then we'd just assume it was part of the fun and games.

'But,' Fiona complained, 'I'm not all that keen about being taken over by that old hag and finding myself floating near the ceiling looking down at my possessed body.'

'I think she only did that to get you here in the easiest possible way.'

'Yeah! And it means having done it once she can do it again. I can't accept that as part of the kinky fun and games.'

'But I can't think why she should ever do it again. I mean she got us both here and that apparently was the point of the exercise.'

Fiona opened her eyes wide and pointed a quivering forefinger at me. 'Point of exercise! But why are we here? I mean – what's it all in aid of?'

I forced her to sit on the bed, then sat beside her and took one shapely hand in mine.

'This is an adventure than cannot have been experienced by many people. Where we are I do not know, but it certainly is not in the world we know.'

If possible her eyes became even rounder. 'You mean we're on another planet?'

'Not exactly. I think we've been taken to another dimension. A place where the princess can do anything she likes. Maybe this house is an extension of her mind.'

'It's all spooky and scary and I want to go home.'

I sighed deeply and shook my head. 'I don't think we can go home unless it pleases the princess to let us. Fiona, don't cry. All this could be very interesting.'

She turned to me while dabbing her eyes with the corner of a bed sheet. 'Interesting! Interesting for you maybe, but horrible for me. I'm sure it's me she wants. And I don't know why.'

I tried so hard to explain, not only to her but also myself, what had taken place, what might take place – and most important – what might never take place.

'We all know deep inside that something like this could happen, has in fact happened to many other people throughout the ages and has been partly recorded in so called mythology. If we think deeply and for a long time we come to understand the world in which we live has been fashioned by our collective imagination, based on information – false or otherwise that has been imprinted on the ancestral mind for countless generations.

'And I am certain there are in our midst special people, those who in mythology were described as heroes, warlocks, gods and immortals. The princess, and in a lesser extent Gredelsa, are such beings.'

Fiona's eyes were bright with tears when she looked up at me and suddenly we were both very lonely; two children lost in a nightmare forest where every tree hid a demon. The fingers of her left hand clawed at my shirt front when she spoke.

'I don't want to even think about such things. I can only remember that I've been violated in the most terrible way. I was driven out of my own body and someone – something – else went in. For something like twelve hours this body was controlled by . . . by a squatter.'

I tried to comfort her. 'It most likely happens to other people quite often, only they don't know it has happened. They talk about blackouts – not being themselves.'

'But I *know*. Have seen. Experienced. And I'm just an ordinary girl who never really had a serious thought in her life.'

'So now you can start thinking seriously. For example. Do

you realise that there is nothing to be seen from any window. I've been watching them ever since we came here. Just green gleaming mist. That probably means this place barely exists in some kind of limbo.'

'And we can never go back to – where we came from?'

'I don't know. Perhaps we never left it. Could be the time-train stands still and it's the scenery that races by.'

Fiona rubbed her hands then blew on them. 'I suddenly feel very cold. Hold me close.'

We were sitting there on the bed, my arms round Fiona's shoulders when there came a tap on the door prior to it opening to reveal a young footman who looked as if he were not more than eighteen years of age. He bowed from the waist and Fiona despite her anxiety, giggled. He had the unbroken voice of an early teenager.

'Madame the Princess requests your presence in the blue room.'

I said: 'Right, lead the way,' but Fiona exclaimed:

'Eh! Hold everything.' Freeing herself from my arms she got up and walked towards the footman. She gave him a dazzling smile and I groaned.

'Now, look here, who are you?'

He gave her another bow. 'James the third footman, if it please you, miss.'

'Oh, come off it. It would please me if you'd let loose with what goes on round here. So far it seems all spooky.'

His clear grey eyes were without expression, his young lineless face without smile or frown. But his voice pronounced each word with clear precision.

'I am not permitted to give information that it not conversant with my duties. Madame the Princess is the font of all knowledge.'

Fiona giggled again and reaching out laid her left hand on his right shoulder. Instantly he vanished.

Fiona stood staring wildly at the space where the young man had been standing, then, without moving, began to cry without sound. Her shoulders shook, tears ran down her face, but there were no gasping cries, no muted sobs. Presently I went to her and took the trembling body into my arms and attempted to explain both to her and myself.

'He was only a projection — I think. We have been conditioned to see what she wants us to see. Our preconceptions are being used to build up our conception of a young footman. I know it sounds complicated — and it is — although at the same time it's extremely simple. Back in our dimension we expect to see a blue sky and green grass because our minds have been conditioned to see just that. In fact I now shudder to think just how much was — is — merely projected images sent out by our brains.'

Fiona struggled to speak and at length managed to do so.

'All I know is — a nice-looking young man was standing there, but when I touched him — and I did for I felt the cloth of his coat under my fingers — he vanished. He wasn't there anymore. And you're saying he was never there. Then we're both going crazy. Oh my God! Perhaps we were always mad.'

Now she began to shake and emit gasping cries so that I was forced to lead her back to the bed and there slap her hard across either side of her face. This had the effect of quelling the hysteria, even though she continued to cry in a normal manner, so that I could comfort to the best of my ability, although heaven above (which it wasn't) knew the only solace I could give was as cold as an icicle at the north pole.

So I wiped her eyes dry on my large red handkerchief — women favour such silly little scraps of material that can be used for nothing more than pat a running nose — and endeavoured to remind her of the non-existent footman's message.

'The princess wants to see us.'

She grabbed my handkerchief and blew her nose into it. 'Well I don't want to see her.'

'Maybe not, my angel, but I still think we'd better go. I'd hate to see her when she's good and truly angry.'

Fiona patted her eyes. 'And I'd hate to see her without a wig.'

'And so would I.'

But Fiona shook her head. 'No you wouldn't. Men are always curious to see horrible things, and I think the princess would look really and truly horrible without that wig.'

'Well then, let's go and see if she's wearing it.'

She shuddered violently when we passed the spot where the

footman had vanished, then clutched my arm when we passed the self-same footman in the hall where he was dusting some picture frames assisted by two colleagues to whom – barring a difference in colouring – he bore a remarkable resemblance.

'No,' I whispered, 'you will not stop to ask him questions. You'll only get I don't-understand-expression and words to match.'

But, as though to give the lie to my words, the footman paused in his task and said in that clear precise voice: 'The blue drawing room is the first door on the left round the corner,' and Fiona thanked him demurely before crying again.

When we reached the door that had been indicated I again handed Fiona my handkerchief and instructed her to wipe her eyes, blow her nose and generally tidy herself up, an instruction I am pleased to record she promptly obeyed. I tapped on the door and on being told to enter by a soft voice, turned the handle and motioned to Fiona to precede me.

Madame the Princess was seated in an immense armchair, attired in a long pale green dress and to my surprise not wearing a wig. Instead her head was completely covered by a dark green shawl or scarf which was fastened in some fashion under her chin.

She motioned us to low chairs which meant we were both forced to look up at her. She smiled at me, then asked in that singularly sweet voice:

'And how are you children coping? This must be very strange to you, particularly the coming and goings of my servants.' She addressed Fiona. 'I can see, my dear, that you have been grievously upset and that I can fully understand. For a young woman like you who has been accustomed since early teenhood to enslave young – and not so young – men with your appearance and sex appeal, to have one disintegrate when you merely touch him, must be an unnerving experience. But comfort yourself by the knowledge he was only make-believe. As your clever young man,' here I was given a swift glance, 'deduced, the entire staff has been created by me to fulfil not only my needs but those of my – guests as well.'

'But your maid, Gredelsa, is she real?' I asked.

'You know very well she is. The one time battle-maiden to the gods is now mine, although I have no need to fight battles these days, she is as real as the thirty-nine universes, as solid as a brick wall.'

'And you, Madame?'

Her eyes blazed and I felt the floor sliding from under my feet; for a moment received a distinct impression that I was poised over a bottomless pit and I was in grave danger of extinction. Then those wondrous dark eyes were gazing upon me with amusement and the voice became tinted with laughter.

'You are becoming almost *too* clever. I mislike a nimble brain that having found a tiny rock of knowledge amidst a sea of conjecture, leaps on to an islet that in turn is but a stepping stone to the main land of truth. Turn down the light in your eyes, young man, and try to emulate your sweet companion whose stupidity is perhaps the most endearing aspect about her.'

I could see that Fiona was not in the least put out by this remark, her one desire being to be dismissed as someone not worthy of attention, a wish I felt certain would not be fulfilled, for it was obvious that although the princess was careful never to look directly at my intended wife, in fact she registered every gesture, every movement and sigh.

'Will you kindly tell me why we have beeen brought to this place?' I requested.

She patted the silk shawl and a bulge that had suddenly appeared, was eradicated. 'We! I have no plans for you at all, for your presence here is to pacify the sweet idiot and keep her reasonably happy. Once she has become acclimatized you will no longer be needed.'

'And Fiona?'

The sudden smile so transformed the princess's face that for a moment I had the impression it was extremely beautiful. She now looked directly at the young girl and nodded very slowly, an action that did nothing to quell Fiona's fears.

'What about Fiona, indeed. Let us say I need a fresh hand-maiden. Gredelsa is far too grim to satisfy all my needs. Tell me, my dear, how would you like to remain young and beautiful for ever? To have the ability to stroll down through the centuries, untouched by the claws of time? This gift I can obtain for you in return for. . .'

Fiona looked up for a moment into the face of the princess,

then lowered her eyes and asked with a shyness I had to assume was not an act: 'In return for what, Princess?'

'In return for your love. Your total love.'

Fiona gasped and slowly shook her head. I knew that in her early teens she had experimented, or perhaps it would be more truthful to admit, had been seduced by an older girl, but fundamentally she was a man's girl with little time for her own sex. The princess's proposal must have both shocked and nauseated her, particularly as the lady now looked both haggard and far from young.

But then I remembered. It was Eve who plucked the forbidden fruit, tempted as she was by the prospect of devastating knowledge. And could any daughter of Eve turn down the prospect of everlasting youth and beauty?

Fiona looked up and I hated the light in her eyes. 'I don't believe you could obtain such a gift for anyone.'

An immense sigh, the suspicion of a tear in the left eye, then the beautiful voice saying:

'I, alas, can do very little for I offended the god and he took back all the gifts he had granted me. But he was not allowed to withdraw that gift which is the birthright of every intelligent being in the thirty-nine universes – hope.

'Listen to me, child. Accept the pure essence of truth: the only thing that need be feared is fear itself. When the Snake God cursed me for daring to give my love to a mortal, he first took back the gift of eternal youth and beauty, but decreed that I would never die. Then he placed upon me that which will make any man born of woman scream in the morass of horror.

'But he was forced to leave me with one tiny spark of hope. When one mortal is found who will love me as I really am, not as I appear to be; when that being can without fear clutch my naked head to his–her naked bosom and still salute my lips with a loving kiss, then will the curse be lifted – all god-given gifts restored. You and I, sweet child, will be young and beautiful together. For all eternity.'

I assumed this tale was intended to be accepted as an allegory, but then I saw the expression depicting intense seriousness on the princess's face, her trembling hands and I felt she had much in common with a man who craves the fulfilment of a long-festering lust. I had to ask the dreadful question.

'What was the curse, Madame?'

Now she bared her teeth in a mirthless grin and I thought of a she-wolf facing a rival over a succulent lamb; her voice had a growling quality.

'You have intelligence, young man, but unfortunately you have also that failing that was the downfall of that four-legged animal most loved by the gods – curiosity. And know you I must reveal the secret to those who request. And I must accept your question as a request.'

My fear became tempered in the fire of courage. 'If you intend to reveal your dread secret, Madame, it is because you have a reason for doing so, not because you must.'

She ignored my remark and turned her full attention to Fiona and after staring at her for some while (which had the effect of making her blush – a minor miracle) then ordered:

'Come here, child.'

And after some hesitation Fiona went to her, trustingly put her hand into that of the Princess Helena and looked into her eyes and listened with sweet gravity as the princess made hesitant speech.

'Would you like to see me as I am, child? Have you the courage to look upon the curse of the Snake God? No. I think you're far too young and inexperienced in the way of the unusual. Let us preserve for a little while the virginal whiteness: may the gods forbid that it be besmirched before it is absolutely necessary.'

But I who had suddenly become jealous of this extraordinary woman, would not let well alone, but must needs taunt and probe the wide-awake tigress until she was stung into unconsidered action – knowing full well I was courting disaster.

'I cannot believe, Madame, that your secret is so dreadful that we cannot look upon it without undue alarm.'

Her eyes again took on a baleful gleam and I tasted the heady drug of fear which had the effect of goading me on to a wilder degree of folly.

She clasped Fiona to her and now I saw the girl struggle weakly and I was again reminded of a pretty bird in the coils of a snake.

'Have you no regard for this girl?'

I nodded. 'Very much so. But I think you are deliberately confusing her by myths.'

'Is this house a myth?'

'It could be. Certainly it is fake. Perhaps you are as well.'

She laughed softly. 'You would like to think so.'

I climbed another rung on the ladder of folly.

'And I certainly think your dreadful curse is fiction. You have confused me with the enigma of Far Acres, but not frightened. Tell me, Madame, is this ghastly secret anything to do with your head?'

She started and pushed Fiona abruptly away so that the girl rolled on to the floor where she lay looking up at the princess with half-fearful astonishment. The clear voice now took on a more pronounced accent and the eyes an element of alarm.

'Why should you think that? Have I ever given you reason to think there is anything wrong with my head?'

'Your answer, Madame, is in the nature of a confession. Apart from which a lady of your cultivated taste would not wear such an outrageous wig unless you had a reason to do so. But now you are hiding your head under a silk shawl – which is oddly disarrayed. . .' Instantly the princess's hands flew like startled birds to her head. 'Not absolutely true, but your so prompt action could again be translated as an involuntary confession. I suspect the loss of hair and possibly an unsightly growth you wish to keep hidden. Understandable, Madame. But would not we three be easier in our minds if the ghastly secret were revealed? Healing follows the surgeon's scalpel.'

Now the fire in her eyes was extinguished and she all but pleaded with me to understand:

'Far Acres is me – and I am as alien to you as fire is to water. I am looking for the one mortal who can love despite the curse that has been set upon me. Fiona may be that person. The sex of the loved one is not important. On the Eternal Road there is no need to divide the life forms into two separate groups. The penis and the uterus are crude physical appendages and have no place on the astral body. But here and now the gods decree and lesser beings strive the best they may.'

'If Fiona is the one you seek, then she should see the worst you can uncover.'

'Later. Let her get to know me first.'

'Imagination will place a monster on a flea's back. Fear if not erased in time will corrode and become terror. Now . . . the never dying Now is the moment of revelation.'

'Suppose she were to turn from me?'

'Then she is not the one you seek.'

After a while Madame the Princess lowered the shawl-covered head and said softly: 'Fiona, my dear, you must remove the scarf – slowly and with care. Remember you have nothing to fear but fear itself.'

My interest was fully aroused for I had not the slightest idea of what was about to be revealed, although I had steeled myself to witness something pretty grim.

I watched Fiona fumble with the knots which kept the shawl in position and felt an irrational impatience when she took longer to do the job than I thought necessary. Then I seemed to live a separate lifetime for each knot to be unravelled, then came the climax when Fiona was at last able to pull the shawl from the princess's head.

Snakes as a growth on the head. Now I knew I had been expecting just that. Every breathing, eating, loving, hating and any other activity that you care to think about had merely been a preparation for the instant in the chain of time when I would see a crop of flesh-coloured snakes writhing, hissing and looking bloody revolting on the head of Her Excellent Highness Princess Helena Landi.

I staggered over to the imitation Adam fireplace and was most violently sick in the hearth. Then I wiped my mouth on a red towel that was suddenly hanging over a chair back and thought that the revolting sight would most likely send Fiona mad. I therefore gave her my full and undivided attention.

She was stroking the bloody things.

Question: When does time reveal the indisputable fact that you are approaching the frontiers of your own lifetime?

Answer: When the girl you near as damn love puts out her pretty fingers with the sole and only intention of stroking flesh-coloured snakes that are rooted in another woman's head.

You see, unknown and most probably non-existent reader, life is run on fear and when your allotted ration has been used up, then it stands to reason your bloody motors must run down. Stop. Become effing cold. Dead.

Soon these fingers that are now flying over these typewriter keys will be turned into powdery ash in a crematory oven. Or is it crematorium? And my brain will boil before causing the skull to explode. Not many people know that. When the fire really gets going the brain boils and then blows a ragged hole in the top of the skull.

Which is fine. Great. No brain – no memory. No nasty mental pictures of a beautiful young girl trying to stroke hissing, gaping-jaw-flesh-coloured-skull-rooted-snakes. Oblivion.

Brother, sister, bisexual, whatever – don't you believe it. Maultravers's essentials may be less than a spoonful of ash, but the vital *him* goes marching on.

How do I know? I can see the land that lies beyond the frontier and there's no sign of non-existence over there. I don't want to remember. . .

I shouted at her: 'Don't. . . In the name of sanity don't touch the slimy things,' and she looked at me with something like love light (whatever that may be) in her lovely eyes and said: 'Don't be silly, Eric, they're beautiful.'

Had there been anything in my stomach to bring up, I'd have been back at the fireplace, instead I merely stood there shaking my head like a fairy saying no to an elf, hearing the princess chuckling away to herself and Fiona sort of crooning a lullaby to the wriggly little horrors.

Finally I waded in with both arms outstretched and grabbed her by the scuff of the neck and dragged her from the room. Madame the Princess's high-pitched laughter followed us.

When the little wretch began to struggle and generally give me a bad time, I slung her over my shoulder, then repeatedly belted her backside with my right hand when she tried to get a fix on my left ear. Once back in our own room I pitched her on to the bed before sitting down for a good think.

CHAPTER TWO

It took some doing. Having a good think. To start with Fiona made several bids for freedom and I had to keep belting her and slinging her back on to the bed. Then I out-shouted her and finally managed to get in a few words.

'She – the princess – has got through to you. She's the snake and you're the bird and she's got a fix on you. I mean to say, would you normally have touched those things? Would you have got within spitting distance of a hissing hair-do?'

She made an effort to speak calmly, but I could see it was quite an effort, as though there was a mental block – such as writers have – that was stopping the words from getting through. Then she spoke with a strange hollow sort of voice, like someone speaking from a vast underground hall.

'The snakes are part of the princess . . . and to touch them is to start a fire that runs all the way up my arms, then down my legs, and then I'm in an awful state so that I want the princess to do dreadful things to me. But under a thick grey blanket of me I'm so frightened and hate the princess so that it would give me pleasure to see her burn . . . No, no, I don't mean that. I wouldn't like to see anyone burn. But if she doesn't, I will . . . or something.'

'Then why do you want to go to her? Keep running away from me?'

'Because she keeps calling to me. To torment, I think. She's stopped now.'

She rested her head on my chest and traced an invisible line down from my shoulder to my hip. 'Now I've marked you sinfully only I don't know how. We'll never find our way back. Only Sarcan the chauffeur can do that and then he has to be driving the car. On foot we'd get lost in the black mists of time.'

'But it won't do any harm to explore this place and try to find

121

out what makes it tick. Last out of doors is a blue-based baboon.'

We ran from my room, down the stairs and out through the front door which was opened for us by a non-existent footman – and a whole crowd of shadows ran with us. Pink gravel crunched under our feet, white rabbits scurried across the path, but we only had eyes for the vast temple with a golden half-coiled cobra on its roof.

The door was open, but it obligingly closed once we were inside; the ceiling was so high a faint golden mist obscured the complicated tracery but in no way dimmed the bright light which came from we knew not where. The walls were covered with gold and silver tiles, each about a foot square and enhanced by a large ruby or emerald. The floor was one immense mirror; green-tinted, but not glass, of that I am certain, and this too reflected the mysterious light that I now think originated from the ceiling.

At the far end – a long way off – stood an altar built of gold bricks, with a gold cobra coiled up on its surface, its expanded hood serving as a background for the glittering rubies that were its eyes. On the front of the altar was embossed the sacred name of the living god:

NETJER-ANKH

'I feel,' said Fiona, 'this is where we came in. You know? Been here before and all that jazz. The Snake God. Must have read about that in lots of pulp magazines and heard its name repeated in lots of old movies. And I'm not all that scared now. I mean – isn't all this tremendous? Here is life unlimited. Just being here does things to you. Can't you feel the power racing through your veins?'

I shook my head sadly. 'No. I feel the cold hand of death poised over us.'

'But I won't really dic,' Fiona insisted. 'I know one can exist outside the body, so what the hell, death is a clot. I'll spit in his face and call him Charlie.'

I gazed at the golden cobra, then round at the temple and it all seemed limitless, a glimpse of that space-time in which universes are born, and I had a foretaste of that terrible loneliness that will come to us all when we at last stand on the edge of the great eternal plain.

I parted with a priceless item of information. 'The god immortalized a mortal woman, gave her many priceless gifts, then tempted her to betray him, knowing she lacked the strength to resist. When she had succumbed he played the game which is so popular among others of his kind – Give and Take and a bonus if a million to one chance comes up.'

'You are,' Fiona said, 'a nasty old cynic. If he can give the princess a crown of snakes he can. . . Well! Look around you – he seems to deal in gold.'

I took her hand and began to pull her towards the entrance.

'To think,' I said, 'this all started by Billie asking for a cup of sugar.'

*

We explored the realm known as Far Acres – as no doubt had others before us – and gradually came to understand it was an artificial world, a few acres claimed from Limbo and furnished from the debris of the princess's mind.

'Even the trees are fake,' I pointed out.

Fiona gripped my mind with mental fingers. 'I bet we could do much better. Wouldn't it be great to make your own world, then create some people who would do exactly what you want.'

I shrugged. 'It's been done before, but the creator soons gets fed up with the entire business. After all it would be like talking to yourself. Little offshoots of self. Boring and rather revolting when you come to think about it.'

'Eric, you think too much. The formula for a happy life: Accept, enjoy and never ask why. So simple. What an idiot the princess must have been to risk losing everything and being clobbered with a head of snakes for a mere man.'

'You wouldn't risk losing all that for me?'

She shook her head so violently for a moment her dark hair looked as if it too might be a nest of writhing snakes.

'Not on your proverbial nelly. I mean let's be honest one day we both might well get over each other – if you understand what I mean.'

'Never,' I promised. 'Not even if I am tempted by Delilah herself and I walk the earth until the sun goes nova.'

She emitted a delightful little chuckle. 'You say that now, but if the princess ever got it all back again and offered you eternal youth and beauty, I'd be brushed aside like nobody's business.'

The young girl in the white muslin dress came out of a hedge – at least she appeared to and stood watching me with deep blue eyes that contrasted nicely with her long auburn hair that was tied by a white ribbon into a pony tail. She was extremely pretty and appealing as she looked up at me from under long lashes.

'Hallo, where did you two come from?'

Fiona clung to my arm and I could almost taste the hostility when I answered:

'I might ask the same of you, for I can't really believe you came through a hedge.'

She put her head on to one side and examined Fiona with great interest. 'But I did. I can come through anything in Far Acres, because nothing is really real, I guess. Do you know something? You're cute. I like cute young men.'

'And I'm rather partial to cute young women. Talking of which may I introduce my fiancée Fiona. And I'm Eric Maultravers.'

The girl did a little mock curtsey and said demurely: 'I'm Katrina. A sort of niece to the princess and looked after by Gredelsa. That makes me kinda important.'

Fiona spoke for the first time and I could see she was not all that taken by the newcomer. 'Do you live in the house?'

Katrina – how well the name suited her – appeared to give this question far more consideration than it deserved, then finally said: 'I'm not sure I *live* anywhere, but if you mean do I manifest in the house, the answer is sometimes. I think if one is asked a simple question one has every right to give a complicated answer. Don't you agree?'

'I think,' Fiona replied rather bitingly, 'that you're over-doing the sweet demure act.'

Katrina widened her blue eyes and transformed her full red lips into a perfect circle. 'Oh! Your claws are sharp, pussy-cat. But isn't it nice for Eric to have two sweet demure pussy-cats? He can watch them growl and scratch and think how desirable he must be to be the cause of such an entertaining war.'

Fiona took a deep breath then released it as a gasp of rage.

'Really, I never –'

'Are you aware,' Katrina interrupted, 'that there is another young man like you wandering around Far Acres? Not necessarily on this time level, but he's here for all that.'

'You're just being plain silly,' Fiona protested. 'Becoming all mystic to attract Eric's attention.'

'It's already attracted,' I stated with great sincerity.

'And what is more,' Katrina continued, 'he is at this duplicated moment in time, reading all about you in a book you're going to write. Well maybe not a great big book, but the equivalent of a long short story. So there, Miss Smarty-Pants.'

Fiona turned to me her eyes sparkling with bitter humour.

'It's this place. It turns out mad people.'

'Correction, you have to be mad to get here. No sane person is allowed through the time mists.'

'Now you're showing off because *she's* here.'

Katrina poked her tongue out. 'He doesn't have to show off. He's sweet as he is. Not a bit like the other one. He's a professional show-off. Not that he isn't dishy in a very expensive sort of way.'

'Then I suggest you go and find him.'

'I'm trying to but the princess has sort of hid him away. She's awfully jealous. You see I've got almost everything she's lost. Youth, beauty and the power to make any man – any mortal man – fall in love with me.'

Fiona did her best to sneer. 'You hate yourself, don't you?'

'No. I love myself. I'm having a wonderful romance.'

Fiona tugged my arm and reluctantly I allowed myself to be pulled away. Back to the house that never was, across ground that had no substance, and back into the hall where a line of make-believe footmen and parlour maids bowed and curtsied as though we were the most royal of royalty.

A plump man attired in conventional black and white who I seemed to have seen in at least two old films, took two steps forward and performed a much deeper bow and after clearing his throat asked: 'Do you feel much better for your constitutional, sir – madam?'

Fiona answered for both of us.

'Yes thank you. But now we feel like a lie down.'

The butler (who else could it be?) did some throat-clearing.

'Just what I was about to suggest, Madam. But before you do so, will you be so kind as to read the note that Madame the Princess has left on the tallboy. It is rather important. Thank you, Sir, Madam.'

Then they all took a step back and vanished.

Fiona expressed her annoyance.

'I'm just about fed up to the back teeth with all this vanishing on the part of the hired help. It's most off-putting.'

I began to propel her towards the stairs. 'Remember they are only projections of the princess's mind, so I suppose in a way it was her telling us to look for a note she has written to us. Probably her sub-conscious doing some over-time.'

Fiona preceded me up the stairs muttering to herself, while I kept my eyes open for any further manifestations. This business of a note worried me, suggesting as it did that the princess had something on her mind she was afraid to tell us about by word of mouth.

We found our room neat and tidy, the bed made up and a green tinted envelope lying on the tallboy.

I held it out to Fiona. 'It's addressed to you. You had better read it.'

She sat on the bed and pouted in an irresponsible fashion.

'Don't want to. I'm fed up to the tits. Read it yourself.'

I tore the envelope open and took out a sheet of green notepaper. I read aloud:

Dear Pretty Child,

Alas it would appear that *He Who Cursed Me* is very displeased with the attention I paid you – including my bringing you both to Far Acres – and so I'm afraid he's going to send something really awful looking for you. And there's nothing I can do or say that will stop him. But darling, please don't blame me. I mean to say, he let me bring Chu-Chu here to play with and I just can't imagine why he has taken off against you like this.

Forgive me if I keep well out of this, but honestly there really is nothing I can do to help. Why not hang on to your boyfriend and refuse to let go, even if that means him sharing whatever is in store for you.

Yours from here to wherever you may be.

Helena.   HEH

Fiona grimaced, pounded rounded knees with clenched fists, then gave utterance. 'She brings me to a place I hate, made advances I did not welcome, then leaves me to face whatever this Netjer-What's-His-Name likes to dish out.'

'Can't think what he can do,' I murmured without any real conviction.

'What about a healthy head of snakes?' Fiona suggested. 'Horror Unlimited.'

I was racking my brain for something comforting to say, when the door opened and a young man poked his head round the frame. He was far too handsome from a masculine point of view, having a smooth olive skin, dark limpid eyes, beautiful white even teeth and a mass of auburn curls that had clearly been dressed by an expert. His light blue suit and hand-painted tie made me grit my teeth. He did not speak so much as purr like a pampered pussy-cat.

'Sorry if I intrude but I seem to have blundered into the wrong time slot. My name is Gore Sinclair but she who speaks calls me Chu-Chu.'

Without waiting for an invitation he entered the room and after giving Fiona a low bow and me a friendly nod, pulled up the nearest chair. Then he produced a gold cigarette case offered it first to Fiona, then myself, before closing it and returning it to his breast pocket.

'Very wise. Giving up the filthy habit myself. I say, we'd better make the most of this as I'm actually trespassing on your time channel and also – just between you and I there's something very nasty waiting for you a little further on. I've just read it up in that account you're going to write.'

I slapped my chest with wide-spread hand. 'What me?'

'You, sir. No one but. Enthralling. Sorry I can't give you any details for that appears to be against the rules. I mean if you knew what was waiting then you'd do something about dodging it and that would muck up the entire business. Might result in the sun going nova a mite early or something. If I make myself clear.'

'You don't,' I retorted caustically. 'Where do you hang out?'

He waved a beautiful hand with exquisite grace. 'Here my

dear fellow, but on a different time level. I've finally got the hang of this time business. I say, you haven't caught a glimpse of a nifty little number called Katrina, have you?'

I nodded. 'Yes, we just left her in the garden.'

He got to his feet and straightened his tie. 'Good. She can belt across the time channels like nobody's business. Must get my hands on the. . . What am I saying? If her ladyship were to hear me there'd be hell to pay. Look here, you won't tell her will you?'

'I won't even mention we've met you,' I promised.

'Good. That's very decent of you. Well, I must try and find my way back. It's a matter of taking the right corners and looking out of the wrong windows. When you can see two separate scenes from adjacent windows, then you're in the wrong time channel. Or is it the other way round? Never mind, follow your nose and you're bound to turn up somewhere.'

He bowed again, examined his reflection in a wall mirror, then left, closing the door softly behind him.

After a silent interval Fiona asked: 'Well, what do you think about that?'

'Me? I've ceased to think about anything, but what about this nasty something waiting for you in the near future? That's two warnings. And I'm going to write about it. Could the princess and her Chu-Chu be having us on?'

'Hope so.'

It was then that the little golden snake dropped on to the bed and slid under a pillow. Fiona screamed and I jerked back for the thought raced across my mind that the bloody thing could have dropped on me. Fiona fell on to the bedside rug and shouted at me:

'Get the finger out – find it and get rid of it.'

I set to with some reluctance for at the best of times snakes are not my favourite animals and the princess's head crop hadn't improved matters.

But I plucked the pillow under which the creature had taken refuge from the bed and released a vast sigh of relief when nothing more lethal than a rolled-up silk stocking was revealed.

'That's not mine,' Fiona protested. 'Green is not my colour.'

'Fine. But where the hell has the bloody thing gone?'

'You'll have to strip the bed.'

That did not take very long as all I had to do was remove a gold colour duvet, matching under sheet, then turn the mattress.

'No gold snake,' I announced.

'Then it must be under the bed.'

I pushed the divan out into the room, turned it upside down, shook all pillows, then thoroughly searched the room. Finally I remade the bed, then repeated the statement.

'No gold snake. That must be the nasty thing that was waiting for us. Well – we've had it.'

Fiona nodded. 'I suppose you're right. I mean she's made us see footmen and maids who don't really exist, so I suppose an imagination-snake would be easy for her to think up.'

'Especially as she was cursed by a snake god and has snakes for hair.'

She sighed deeply and began to undress. 'Well it's not here, so we must have been made to see a gold snake. But I'm not happy. Not happy at all. Why do I feel so tired?'

I stiffled a yawn. 'Me too. But of course we must have a right to feel tired, what with your body being possessed and me rushing around trying to find out what this is all about. A thought – is sleep real in this place? I mean you could just imagine you're asleep but in fact be stumbling around in the mists of time.'

Naked, Fiona slid under the duvet and I from pure force of habit moved in beside her. 'I suppose,' I began hopefully, 'you wouldn't. . .?'

'You are joking! How does one put the light out in this place?'

I sat up and looked at the ceiling. So far as I could see the light came from where ceiling met walls even though there was no light strip.

'I think you have to think it out.'

I could see Fiona nod her head sleepily. 'OK. I *think* the light out.'

Instantly darkness annihilated every speck of light and I sank back on to the pillow and allowed a torrent of nasty thoughts to pour through my brain, most of which were based on the concept of a golden snake that had disappeared under a pillow and had looked much too solid to be merely a product of a super-imagination.

Suddenly Fiona's voice came from beside me: 'Funny how the light went out like that, almost as if it – the light – wanted to go out and only used my thinking as an excuse.'

My hand finally found hers and I felt a little happier. 'That sounds very complicated. More than it really is.'

'I can't help that. The point is I've been trying to think it back on again, but have had no joy.'

I thought very hard. 'Well, that must be because you don't really want it back on.'

A long pause during which her hand tightened its grip on mine. Then: 'I'm not going to worry about it. No more than I'm worrying about a gold snake that was never found. Let's think ourselves asleep.'

'Let's do that.'

And in no time at all we were both asleep.

*

I did not at first know why I woke suddenly; because all at once I was wide-awake, every sense alert; the short hairs on the back of my neck standing erect, a condition up to that time I would not have thought possible. I lay perfectly still and listened; my ears strained to detect the faintest sound. Far away there came the haunting cry of an owl or some night creature, then the sound died away and a dreadful silence descended upon the darkness; became part of it, pressed down on me, and I was very cold as if I was sharing the bed with a block of ice, then when I started to think the light on, the sound began, or rather restarted, for I knew now this was the reason for my sudden awakening.

The fear and the cold held me in an icy grip and I could only lie still and try to think of a rational explanation. And how quickly I grabbed the conjectual straw. Snoring! That was it. Fiona was snoring. The sound grew louder. I defined it gradually, taking each part in turn and trying to make a pattern of the whole. First there was a drawing-in; a slightly hoarse, breath-gasping gurgle, then a harsh, obscene blowing out. This was followed by an entirely unexplainable slithering like dough being rubbed on a pastry board; then the process was repeated, only now somewhat faster. The pattern was complete when I placed the combination of sounds in their right category. It was a sucking noise, as though a baby with an abnormal appetite and an outsized pair of lips, was taking nourishment from a feeding bottle. Once the bed trembled slightly and I reached out for Fiona's hand.

'Wake up, Fiona,' I said just above a whisper, 'you're snoring like hell.'

I found her hand, just where I had released it earlier: it was cold, very bony and felt as if it were loosely wrapped in silk. An icy shiver raced up my body and I screamed:

'Light! In the name of sanity let there be light.'

And there was light. The darkness exploded; it was shattered into a thousand splinters; the wreckage lay all around the room, a rectangular shadow under the dressing table, a broken slab of darkness on one side of the wardrobe, a long smear over the wainscoting; all else was light. I really did try to understand, fought to repel the bitter bile that rose to my throat, while I stared at the thing that was coiled round the dressing table, curved gracefully down to the floor; a long white length that rippled gently; and at places rubbed its white roundness against the wall, then curled into a loop, its extremity hidden from sight by the bed. It was all of forty feet long and perhaps a foot in diameter; a long flesh-coloured snake; the great-great-great-grandfather of those that had their origin on the princess's head. Covered with a beautiful white delicate skin, such as might adorn a woman's shoulder. In places there was a faint pink flush; a sign of health on a smooth cheek or perhaps an emblem of modesty, dawning love, or anger; on the white snake those coyish pink hues were the final epitome of obscenity. I sought blindly for Fiona's shoulder, alive to a need to share this nightmare, but my fingers only found a pillow still crumpled and hollow where her head had rested. But Fiona had gone; was down there on the floor – with that thing.

I cried out and as though in answer a head came up over the edge of the bed; a round caricature of Fiona's face, smoothly veined like a gooseberry, with thick pink negroid lips that were parted displaying a line of toothless gums. From between gaping jaws came a roaring shriek such as one might expect from a king cobra – and I had the ridiculous feeling it did not like the light and I was being ordered to *think* it out.

I rolled over to Fiona's side of the bed and looking down saw her lying on the bedside rug, her face was turned away, the dark hair disarranged and she looked like a broken doll discarded by a destructive child.

I reached down and touched her shoulder and called out: 'Fiona, are you all right? Can you hear me?'

The crumpled figure did not stir, so I pushed her gently and she rocked slightly as though half-asleep, annoyed at being disturbed, until she collapsed into a network of creases and ridges. Then I shook even harder – and her head jerked over and I was staring at a skull loosely covered with white skin. She was nothing more than a pile of bones in a skin bag; a deflated balloon; a hideous bundle. The essence of Fiona, that which had manifested as a beautiful body, that lay stretched out across the floor, thumping its soft roundness on the carpet.

I rose and stood upright and stared with well-controlled fear at the flesh-snake and shouted my horror, my rage, only restrained from attacking it with clawing hands by the knowledge it would be Fiona's flesh that would be hurt, a thought that made my stomach heave.

Instead I stood and cursed Madame the Princess, damned her Snake God who had so horribly taken my love from me, then sank to my knees and took skin-clad bones into my arms and tried to smooth tousled hair, all the while praying: 'Don't ever leave me. Take on whatever form, but never leave me.'

The great white flesh-snake pushed the parody of Fiona's face against the door and at once it slid open so that the vile creature could slither from the room – and the awful thought came to me that her ego might be trapped in that serpentine body – and I dropped the sagging, fleshless body, ran to the door and was in time to see the undulating white length at the far end of the corridor. It raised its head and looked back at me – but I could not believe Fiona, the girl I had loved for so long, was behind those blank protruding eyes. No, that was nothing more than a grotesque toy created for a god's amusement; a thing that from being small, became big by feeding on the flesh of a lovely young girl.

I screamed after it: 'Become nothing. Go into oblivion.'

The head turned away, the body disintegrated into a thin stream of golden dust; a cold wind blew along the corridor and the gold dust became yellow mist that drifted away.

When I returned to the room that had been ours Fiona's grisly remains had disappeared.

I began to write an account of everything that had taken place since that ill-fated engagement party. I will continue to do so to the very end.

CHAPTER THREE

Madame the Princess sent for me when the light went out of its own accord and what did duty for sunlight turned the windows into silver-gold rectangles. To my surprise her eyes were swollen as from prolonged weeping and she greeted me with kindly concern.

'My poor friend! How I feel for you. I too had come to love her and it was never my intention that you two should ever be parted. Instead I had hoped we might make a loving threesome. But *he* the god has these dreadful whims. He must have thought the lovely girl would bring me a modicum of happiness, possibly come to love me *for* my curse, not in spite of. It was when she came to stroke *them* he became enraged. Of that I am certain. Certain.'

'Was it necessary to send that thing?' I demanded, for I could not dismiss the thought she was at least partly responsible for the flesh-snake, but she merely shook her head and allowed tears to run down her face unchecked.

I tell you it was not my wish. The white snake is just one of the manifestations the god can take. But I need your help. In fact I must have it. Come and sit by me.'

I spoke in the harshest tones I had yet employed when addressing her, but Fiona's death had removed any fear for my own safety; I might not welcome death, but from now on I would not trouble to remove myself from its path.

'I will not help you under any circumstances, Madame. Please send me back to my own world.'

'If and when you have done what I require.'

'If you need help why not call upon your friend, Gore Sinclair.'

She looked up her eyes bright with tears. 'Chu-Chu! You have seen Chu-Chu? But how can that be? You are on different time channels.'

I shrugged. 'It would seem from what he told me, he had blundered on to ours. He knew what was going to happen to us from reading an account I am going to write.'

The grief was swiftly replaced by anger and the light in her eyes transformed into a soul-freezing glare.

'The fool. I warned him to keep away from that girl. She takes perverse pleasure in leading innocents astray, knowing by now every wayward pathway that is masked by a rose bush, or crooked road that can be reached by means of a crooked path. Call upon him, you say? If he is ever seated upon a throne it will be because I placed him there. Why must I give my heart to a fool?'

I smiled in a manner I liked to think of as grim, but was possibly only mildly sardonic.

'Those who consider themselves great often do, Madame. But I again repeat, I cannot help you.'

'But you must. In fact you are the only person who can. Our friend, our sweet, lovely Fiona. Her body was adapted, but she . . . she still lives.'

It was then I came truly alive for I shouted: 'What?'

'Yes, indeed. Death can find no place in Far Acres and so the essential Fiona lives on. In appearance she will have aged twenty years or more for the white snake took his due and her new temporary body will be without substance so there can be no contact between you – not even speech. Sign language maybe.'

'But I will be able to see her?'

'Yes, when and if you find each other, but be prepared for a change. Think of her as she would have been at forty.'

'I don't care what she looks like. I'll see her . . . make some sort of contact.'

The princess grimaced. 'Yes, sometimes. But I greatly fear Fiona, like you, will blame me for her sudden transformation. She will have the power to haunt me. I want you to seek her out and explain in any way you can I had no part in the unfortunate incident.'

'But you did, Madame. If you had not kidnapped Fiona – or rather her body – neither of us would be here and so would not have been in danger of offending your Snake God. So I will not under any circumstances encourage Fiona to ease up on you. I hope she gives you hell.'

The princess drummed a quick tattoo on her knee. 'And I would ensure you had hell, my friend. Share my curse for example. It can be so easily done. I can will you to place your hands on my naked head – or plunge your face into my nest after ensuring the little dears are fully aroused. I think you will do as I ask.'

'But Fiona will be both frightened and angry. She will never leave you because I ask her.'

'She will when she comes to understand your predicament. When she has been convinced I am not to blame for the visitation.'

I am not a brave man. In fact under certain circumstances I might well be shown up as a coward. Most people are fortunate they rarely if ever are called upon to act against the most basic instinct which was intended to warn the body it is in danger of being hurt or even destroyed. That basic instinct is fear. It is right to heed the warning and remove the body from the danger area, but for centuries it has been considered honourable and heroic not only to remain in the danger area, but actually force the shrinking body into it. Place oneself in the cannon's mouth, bravely go to meet the machine gun bullets.

And now duty – shades of Nelson, Captain Oates, Grace Darling and that stupid little wretch who insisted on remaining on the burning deck merely because his father had told him not to move – demanded I back Fiona's quite justified vengeance campaign and thus get myself a fine crop of flesh snakes.

She watched me leave the room, indeed her eyes were on me as I turned to close the door, and I instantly began to look for what was left of Fiona, not knowing if she would appear for there was always the chance the princess for some obscure reason, had lied to me. Nevertheless I would go on searching until I dropped.

The task was made even more complicated by the rooms changing as I either entered or left them, so I could never be certain which ones I had seen. I can only suppose the princess wanted me to keep my strength up for after I had more or less stumbled into the library for the third time, the dining room had replaced it on the fourth.

Helena was seated at the far end of the table; she was dressed in a long black robe with a matching woollen shawl covering her head.

She motioned me to a chair to her right. 'You poor boy. All that fruitless walking from one room to another with not a sign of our pretty shade. I have arranged for a nice steak and kidney pie to be served. That will enrich your blood.'

A footman served me. Steak and kidney in rich gravy occupied one half of the plate, chopped cabbage and small boiled potatoes the other half; a slice of flaky pastry over-lapped cabbage and meat. A glass of white wine stood on a little round mat to my right.

The princess ate nothing at all. I pushed aside an empty plate and it was instantly replaced by one containing apple pie and custard. My wine glass was refilled – twice. White coffee completed the meal.

I then asked a very pertinent question.

'Madame the Princess, was the meal I have just eaten real or an illusion created by your mind?'

The princess smiled mischievously. 'Do you feel as if you have eaten non-existent food?'

'No I feel well fed. There's even a touch of indigestion.'

'You will find a glass of bicarbonate of soda to your left.'

'Therefore I can only assume someone has been cooking. And as the staff are only images and you are not what I would call a cooking lady, I must be digesting the results of Gredelsa's culinary skill.'

She nodded smilingly. 'You could be right. Now are you ready to continue your search?'

I nodded. 'Yes, until I find her.'

The princess leaned back in her chair and looked at me from sad eyes. 'Wouldn't it be more sensible and kinder to your feet if you sat still and waited for her to come to you?'

'I hadn't thought of that.'

'No, like my Chu-Chu you are inclined to make simple tasks difficult and difficult ones impossible. If I were you I'd wait in the room you both used. She'll find her way there sooner or later. In fact she may be there already.'

I was on my feet almost before she had finished speaking: on my way to the door I stopped and looked back. 'This will make no difference, I won't ask her not to haunt you.'

'It is not all that important. The girl who has become a ghost-woman will trail me like a starving wolf, but there is always you for me to torment. But go to your room and wait in the never ending now.'

I waved my hand as an impatient gesture and left the room slamming the door with unnecessary violence behind me. When I looked back the door had disappeared and had been replaced by a wall with a black gate painted on it.

When I got back to my room it too had undergone a startling change. It had become our bedroom in our flat back in St John's Wood. It was then, for the first time in my adult life I cried real tears, not only for the passing of Fiona but the demise of my own youth. For our love had come into being in that golden country where the sun never sets and the total population never exceeds the magical number of two.

I opened the door and went into the sitting room, then through another doorway and on to a landing which was flanked by a small kitchen on one side and the bathroom on the other. But when I opened the main door it was to look on to the Far Acres corridor.

I went back to the bedroom and found that all of Fiona's clothes were still hanging in the largest wardrobe and folded neatly in the drawers. An army of shoes and knee-high boots were lined up ready for walking orders in one lowboy, their heels resting over a chromium-plated rail.

Here Fiona still lived in a very abbreviated form; a ghost built of memories, perfume, essence of clothes, shoes and hair brushes, plus personality debris.

I went back into the living room and sank down into her armchair, then closed my eyes.

Her voice was a little above a whisper: 'You idiot, Eric. Don't say you're mourning for me?'

I dare not open my eyes or move so much as an inch lest I destroy the, as yet, slender, frail link, but I answered in a loud whisper and in the same mocking style.

'Why should I mourn for you? Now I'm free to go chasing the birds, get flaming drunk every Friday night and generally have a good time.'

There was a long pause and I began to think that maybe the dream had dispersed, when she spoke again.

'Just like you. Callous, unfeeling brute. If you had been gobbled up by a monster snake I would have wept for a full five minutes. I might even have given up strong drink for a few days.'

'You always had a heart of gold – solid all through.'

'Ha, ha, ha, very funny.'

Another pause during which I racked my brains in an effort to think up something to say, that eventually was broken by Fiona's voice breaking into a cry of anguish:

'Oh, Eric! I miss you so much and it's so horrible floating about in this place where nothing is real. You do realise you're not really in our flat? It's all been dreamed up by *Her*.'

I found I was crying again but still able to ask the all important question: 'Will I be able to see you again?'

'Uh-uh. If you concentrate really hard and I do the same, you'll see me most of the time. But I won't be like the old me. I've aged quite a bit.'

'The princess said you would have.'

'That makes me want to cry again. To have my youth taken from me before I really had time to enjoy it – that's awful.'

'But, Fiona you were twenty-four.'

'Don't be so horrid. Twenty-four is cradle age.'

'The princess will fix it for you to have eternal youth if you will only agree she had nothing to do with –'

There was an explosion behind me, a terrifying cold blast that made my hair stand on end, then a much older Fiona was standing in front of me her eyes blazing with hate. Her voice had become deeper, almost masculine when she spoke.

'I'll haunt that woman till the day when the sun becomes a red balloon – and then I'll really get started. Hot iron balls under the armpits, freezing iron pineapples between the thighs –'

'Fiona, I can see you! Solid as a London bus! You're standing in front of me wearing a green velvet dress that contrasts nicely with a ruby necklace.'

This announcement caused her to stop in mid-sentence and for a while she seemed only capable of staring at me with gaping mouth and glazed eyes. Then:

'Don't lie. How old do I look?'

I knew that to be a loaded question and I must be very

careful as to which one of several possible answers I gave. Finally I came up with what had to be a masterpiece.

'Maturely young.'

Of course it did not satisfy: 'That means I look bloody old. Really bloody old. Thank you very much. I'm very grateful to you for being so brutally honest. Sagging muscles, baggy eyes, a face like a road map. . .'

'Will you shut up?'

'Wait until I get my hands on that bitch. Just wait. And that old hag Gredelsa. Hell! I don't look like her do I?'

I raised my voice for apart from appearance Fiona did not seem to have altered all that much.

'Look I'm going to be absolutely honest. You –'

'That means he's going to be really brutal.'

I shut my eyes, took a deep breath, then let her have it. 'You look like a beautiful dark lady of around forty.'

'In other words, an old hag.'

'A very attractive dark lady in her prime. At the very peak of her beauty.'

'Balls.'

'And it's a source of great grief to me that I can't lay my hands on you. I can't – can I?'

She shook her head. 'No. I'm only loosely held together and would come apart at the seams if you were to so much as breathe on me. It's my great hate which keeps me going. Of that I'm certain. Do you know what I'd really like to do?'

'No. What?'

'Send that snake-thing after her.'

'How would you do that?'

'I don't know. But I'd like to do it.'

I sat watching her for some time until I gradually realised that she was becoming unsubstantial; slightly misty round the edges, then put into words what I instinctively knew to be the truth.

'Fiona, listen to me and don't get all hysterical, for that's bad for your state of being. Shortly the princess will put paid to me. In fact I can't understand why she hasn't done so long ago. But I'm writing down everything that has happened to us and I'm going to leave it in the library where that gigolo fellow can find it. For if there's one thing of which I am certain, he's a survivor.

He'll finish up sitting on the very top of the muck heap. But me
– I'm for the chop.'

'Then you'll come and join me.'

I shook my head. 'No, Angel, I fear not. I'm too ordinary. No
great gift, a first time rounder. I've no place reserved for me
among the gods. When I go I'll finish up in the melting pot and
most likely emerge as part of twelve other people. See what I
mean?'

Her outline was now quivering but her voice remained clear.

'I won't allow that to happen. It mustn't. If there's immortality ahead I want you with me. It might be fun then.'

'Fiona, it will never be fun. Death is the reward for living;
without that prospect life will become a vice that grips the soul
between vicious claws. But once I have gone you will soon
forget what I looked like. That will be the tragedy.'

Her face became convulsed and there was fear in her eyes;
her form shimmered and I called out to her, hoped with all my
being she would hear and obey.

'Fiona, take strength from me. Absorb my essence before the
princess erases me from the time spectrum. Please do as I ask –
command. Let my dissolution be a last act of love.'

She passed from my sight but I could still detect her presence
in every part of the room. Also I became aware of a slight
weakening of my senses: a gradual draining of my life force. At
heart Fiona was a practical person.

Then our sitting room changed abruptly into the bedroom
we had shared in Far Acres and I heard the princess calling to
me:

'Has she come to you yet?'

And I called back with something like joy in my heart: 'Yes,
Madame, she has come to me, but now she has gone, but
greatly stronger than she came.'

Suddenly the princess was standing in front of me, her face a
hideous mask of anger and alarm. Her hand became a brief
flash of bright light and the cover flew from her head, revealing
the writhing nest, the tiny gaping jaws, the thin-stubby pink
bodies interwoven, hissing, cotton-thin red tongues flickering;
microscopic red eyes gleaming. But they could not match the
glare which came from Madame's eyes. And the head snakes
became still when she spoke.

'You fool! You have given her the power to haunt me. Yes, she will follow me, a change of dress colour signifying a fluctuating time division, and she is at this moment feeding on your dying body, but I'll soon be paid to that. I will send the white snake to you. It will come as a shadow, become a beautiful gold snake, then grow up. . . But you know what to expect.'

I nodded. 'Yes, indeed I do and strange as it may seem, coward though I be, I'm not afraid. But I would ask one last favour, Madame.'

She raised an eyebrow. 'Ask away.'

'It is this, will you kindly send – your friend to the library. I have a few more paragraphs to write.'

She nodded smilingly. 'Your favour is granted.'

*

I am writing these last lines in the library and the princess has kept her promise. The little gold snake is under the table with its fangs sunk into my ankle. But thankfully Fiona hasn't left a great deal for that thing to grow fat on. I can hardly hold the pen and soon . . . very soon . . . I'll be sleeping the big. . . .

III

Account Given by Gore Stephen Sinclair

CHAPTER ONE

I did read the manuscript from cover to cover after all, but I can't pretend it made me any more cheerful. Now I know what my fate will be if I upset My Lady. I also know now who the dark lady was – and what she was. In a strange way, by even stranger means, the threads were being drawn together to form a most weird pattern. The ensuing picture would confuse the eye and set fire to the brain.

The cloud of fantasy were forming shapes that conformed to the rules of a yet-to-be-considered reality. God and devil shared one throne and worked miracles on alternate days. Or maybe every other Sunday.

I, Gore Stephen Sinclair, off-spring of an illustrious family, gigolo, author most extraordinary, adventurer, traveller of the time ways, was being gradually, subtly transformed into something that belonged to the pages of the wildest fiction. This I knew, even if I was as yet incapable of turning this knowledge into words.

And there was Katrina. Since reading Eric Maultravers' manuscript I keep confusing her with Fiona, even though they have little in common. But that sweet child-woman always seems to appear whenever I think of her – which is quite often – then disappears when my brain sort of screams at her.

That's a fact. If she starts being a nuisance – and in a way I can't understand – I can get shot of her by *thinking her away*.

Katrina was seated on the other side of the table when I finished reading the manuscript. She poked her tongue out and said in a sing-song:

> He read all Eric had to say,
> And now doesn't know which way,
> He must go to break free,
> From the nasty Lady Landi.

She made a face: 'Sorry that's the best I can do. I'm not awfully good at narrative poems.'

'Katrina, who are you exactly?'

'Your dream girl that you have never met. No . . . no . . . no much more. I mustn't think of who I really am. You must find out!'

'And the princess – who is she?'

'The Ultimate. The eternal-mother-mistress-protector-rewarder-punisher-lady-in-distress.'

'Enough,' I protested. 'And who is Netjer-Ankh?'

She clasped her hands together and formed her lips into a perfect red ring and emitted a long drawn out: 'O. . .o . . .o . . .o. That is a dreadful question. No one is certain who he is. You can only guess – and most likely be wrong. His real name is unknown and would be unpronounceable if it were. Maybe he doesn't know who he is. Let's go into the temple. I feel foolhardy and brave today.'

I followed her through the back doorway and into the flower garden. The temple reared up against the pink sky and above it did seem as if the gold cobra peered down at us with baleful disfavour, as though we were intruders who had no business to disturb the divine tranquillity. When I stepped through the open doorway and entered the temple, I was again astounded by the immense size that was not even suggested by the exterior and the mysterious source of light that seemed to radiate from the high ceiling.

Katrina led me towards the altar on which was embossed the god's name.

NETJER-ANKH

And it was here that she first sank to her knees, then lay flat upon her stomach, her arms and legs stretched out until she had assumed a posture that resembled an X cross. The mirror floor reflected me looking down at a body that was suspended over a dazzling sea of light, until that light gradually faded and we were both marooned in a golden twilight. And it did seem as if the cobra on the altar had turned its head and was looking down at the prone supplicant. A voice spoke and it took some little while for me to realise that it was Katrina's.

'. . . listen to me I pray, and grant to me the gift of individual life so that I can be to him she who he desires. Let me not be lost in the sea of power, let me know true ecstasy if only for a little while.'

Her voice ceased to intone its prayer and the light quivered as though about to fade completely, before that voice I had heard before – sexless, calm, yet exciting, filled the temple and sent its vibrating echo down the avenues of time.

'By mortal were you created and therefore owe no allegiance to me, neither can I grant you boon or favour. Rather must you merge with the source from which you sprung.'

Katrina raised her voice to a piteous cry before she again pleaded: 'No. I would be myself and create my own AM.'

Now the voice contained a hint of anger. 'Your desires border on blasphemy. We turn our face from you.'

The light rose up to its former brightness as I helped to raise a softly crying Katrina, then led her back to the slowly opening door and I lacked the courage to ask her for information concerning her prayer to the Snake God and the reason for its refusal.

When we came to the back door of the house she straightened up and looked anxiously over one shoulder.

'I will go back to the place that apparently I can never leave, accept the princess's strictures for no purpose will be served by my defending my action. Now, dry my tears for they were shed for your sake, then kiss me for we may not meet again.'

I found a new red handkerchief in my pocket and with this I did indeed dry her tears, then kissed her long and hard on the lips; and I experienced that joy which only comes when the first tender longing of early youth is sated, even though some vital emotion was missing.

Then Katrina broke free from my arms and went running back across the garden, only to merge into a beautiful blue-rose tree – that in turn disappeared from sight.

When I entered the house a footman was waiting in the hall; he bowed deeply and said with a clear young voice:

'Madame the Princess demands your presence in the blue drawing room, sir.'

I thought myself into the blue drawing room, there found Madame the Princess seated in a vast armchair, wearing a green robe and matching head shawl. She motioned me to a footstool that seemed to crouch like a large marmalade cat near her feet.

'Be seated, Chu-Chu, in the only place that is yours by right when in my presence.'

When I was in a position that forced me to look up at her, I realised that never before had she looked so old, haggard and ill. Only the magnificent eyes still remained both beautiful and ageless, as indeed – I observed a little later – did the hands. Her eyes took on a bleak expression when she spoke.

'So, Chu-Chu, you disobeyed me. You allowed that conniving little wretch to lead you into the temple, then stood silent when she pleaded with the god to give her full life and freedom. And,' here a sardonic smile did not enhance her face, 'how her tears flowed when he turned his face from her. She suffers now as I never did.'

I frowned and dared to glare at her.

'You are very vicious, Madame, to one who is without power, save that given by virtue.'

How my lady laughed. Put back her head, opened her mouth so wide I could see all the perfect white teeth; screwed up her face until the eyes had well nigh disappeared and literally shook with laughter. Finally the green shawl became displaced and a tiny diamond-shaped, pink head slid down over her forehead, only then did she regain self-control and pointed a shaking forefinger at me.

'Virtue! That simpering little fool wearing the white crown of virtue! Under that demure surface there bubbles a lake of seething lust. Lust for life, freedom and lust for you, Chu-Chu the beautiful. Lust for pleasure, lust for pain.'

She lapsed into silence and I watched the anger fade from her face, to be replaced by an expression of sadness. Then she looked down at me.

'Chu-Chu, you must leave me. It is so ordained if I am to be set free, you must take a journey through the underworld. Alas, it is a fearsome place and I have no way of knowing if you will arrive at the divine destination. Yes, my Chu-Chu, you must cross the underworld to reach the dwelling place of the immortal gods. And, Chu-Chu, the underworld is sometimes called Hellvonia.'

'How do I enter this – underworld?' I asked.

'Just by opening that door. The entrance to Hellvonia is on the other side. Goodbye, Chu-Chu, I hope we meet again.'

When I arrived at the door (the one by which I had entered the room) I hesitated. I looked back at the princess. She looked even more dismal and I could only suppose she really did regret my departure.

'Is it really necessary for me to take this journey?'

'Absolutely necessary, Chu-Chu.'

*

When I opened the door of the blue sitting room I fully expected to step out into a fire and brimstone hell, instead I found myself in an ordinary corridor lit by green-tinted windows, which however seemed to stretch out forever on both sides. Windows that merely permitted the entry of green light, but did not allow me to see anything more than a green mist that hid what ever scene there may have been beyond. I remembered the black-time mist and wondered vaguely if this green variety served some similar purpose. To enable hideous beings to exist and manifest under peculiar conditions.

Apart from a doorway from which I had just emerged, the opposite wall was an unbroken green expanse and again I had occasion to ponder on the significance of green. Nature's colour. Could it be that Far Acres existed – so far as it existed at all – in some dimension that depended on and was part of green grass, leaves and any other vegetable life form? Cut down trees and destroy an universe.

Left seemed to be the correct way in Far Acres, so I went left, began to walk: to begin an endless journey between windows and wall. A white-green-tinted floor, matching ceiling, green mist illuminated windows on my right, green painted wall on my left. A green passageway carved out of Limbo – or maybe a vast privet hedge – or the interwoven branches of a forest roof.

To walk and appear to stand still. To see only two walls and a line of windows. This was a a level of hell that Dante had not imagined. The complete absence of sound became unbearable. When I shouted WHY? the three letter word went echoing both forward and backward, then came thundering back to explode in my brain.

WHY?

The most terrible small word in any language because it lights a spluttering fuse that will eventually undermine that citadel that man with rare optimism has called Faith.

Faith can never survive when bombarded by the arrows of enquiry. As time does not exist when there are no means of measuring it, I may have walked for an hour, a day – a year. But suddenly I was opposite a red door set in the left wall and such was my relief it did not occur to me to wonder what might lie beyond, I merely grabbed the cut-glass handle and flung the door open.

A red room. Red floor, ceiling, walls, with flames painted in a deeper red over the fireplace which somehow suggested they were part of the roaring fire that blazed in the grate below.

A young man lounged in a plain wooden chair before the fire, and he turned his head and looked at me with such an air of almost painful boredom, I felt compelled to stifle a yawn.

A beautiful young man with flowing black hair and a long white face lit by large black eyes. He was dressed in a black satin tunic and matching trousers. Black velvet slippers covered his slender feet, while a large ruby glittered on the third finger of his left hand.

He clicked his fingers and another chair that corresponded with his own appeared on the other side of the fireplace. His voice sounded like breaking milk chocolate.

'Sit down, dear boy. And welcome to the Underworld.'

I was grateful to rest my feet although the rest of me did not feel particularly tired. The fire gave out an intense heat, but when I drew my feet back the young man again clicked his fingers which resulted in the fire dimming down to a pile of red hot ash.

I asked: 'Who are you?'

His beautiful long fingers quivered then were still: 'That is a question I have asked myself for a very long time. I am lord of the snakes but that doesn't mean all that much. The creature who sent you here was once my mistress – is that term still in use? – but she is now under my severe displeasure. Good Whatshisname, she gave me a pair of horns.'

I remembered the voice in the temple, the thing which came for Fiona – and shrank back in my chair.

The beautiful white face assumed a semblance of a smile. 'I

have my playful moods, but a god must be allowed certain diversions.'

Greatly daring I asked: 'Can you define the difference between a god and a monster?'

He laughed long and low which he presently terminated by speech.

'As you have probably been told, power corrupts and absolute power corrupts absolutely. Absolute rot. But it does mean one is apt to become a trifle careless at times. Even callous. Yes, I suppose you could class me – and my colleagues – as a monster. The dreadful things I have done in the name of duty would make your hair curl.'

Scarcely had he finished speaking than a small golden snake dropped on to the hearth. I could not restrain a loud cry, but the young man merely seized the small reptile between the jaws of a pair of tongs and dropped in on the fire. There was a spurt of flame and the creature disappeared.

He replaced the tongs on a brass hook then continued.

'Do you know, I sometimes allow myself to be persecuted? Most of us do. It makes us feel good, knowing we can blast the persecutor at anytime we wish. But I cannot believe Helena – as she calls herself these days – will be happy with the thought of you sitting here talking to me. The little gold snake could have been a gentle hint for you to get moving. And after all there is much for you to see and experience.' He got up with every sign of reluctance and pushed his chair back, before spitting into the fireplace. Instantly the fire was transformed into a heap of grey ash.

'Mustn't waste fuel,' he murmured. 'It's so difficult to get these days. After you, dear boy.'

The door slid open and we emerged out into the corridor which now seemed to curve slightly in the far distance, both before and behind; but the atmosphere seemed to have changed since I left it, become much colder, there being condensation on the windows. This became more dense as we progressed until the windows were frosted panels, while water dropped from the ceiling and formed little pools on the floor.

Then I came to realise that the floor was sloping downwards and a green fungus covered the walls and later on the windows until we were slowly walking along a foul-smelling lane that was partly lit by means of green illuminated discs that were fitted to the ceiling every ten yards or so. The young man – he ignored my request for his name – walked on my left, his right hand gripping my arm; a grip that tightened whenever I attempted to walk faster or slower. But his voice suggested nothing but a kind of amicable politeness and even went so far as to apologize (somewhat off-handedly) when I complained of the cold and damp which was doing nothing for my general comfort.

'Please forgive our shortcomings but we have so little to work with and water is something we cannot possibly do without. But you'll soon be warmed up – in one way or another.'

I was not too happy about the last remark but decided it would be wiser to face each experience as it came and not worry about what may be waiting in the future. But what with dripping water which was beginning to take on the attributes of a light shower, the coldness and the increasingly slippery floor, I was finding the journey heavy going, and giving way to a blast of anger snatched my arm from the young man's grasp and grabbed his instead.

'Now,' I stated, 'if one of us slips, both will finish up on the floor.'

'Ground,' he corrected. 'We left the floor behind some while ago, we are now walking over ground. Earth, dirt, sand and a lot of water. You will note it is pouring down. Rain.'

I saw a thin green snake slither under a small bush and shuddered.

'Are we still in Far Acres?'

He helped me clamber over a rock barrier.

'No, of course not. These are the outskirts of Hellvonia. Or the Underworld if you prefer. Hell was transferred to the world you know long ago. But don't get down-hearted, it's very grim here in places.'

The transformation took place at once. A black and white land. The close-clipped grass was black, so was the sky. The flowers which grew in thick clusters in round beds, were white – so was the moon. It was also at least three times as large as the one I remembered; a mighty white orb, set in a velvet black starless sky; the craters and mountains standing out like erupted veins on the face of a dying man.

'The garden of misery,' the young man explained. 'A bad beginning for a dreadful journey. Black stands for depression, white for unfulfilled hope, the worse possible kind. The enlarged moon will give you clear vision.'

A short walk under an alien sky where the only sound was the tramp of my own feet and the dull thud of my heart. Then tall black iron gates glided back to reveal a scene that will never be erased from my living brain.

I was looking down the length of a broad valley which was flanked on either side by tall, fire-tipped mountains. Never had I in the wildest flight of imagination dreamed of such a horror-ridden, gloomy place. Black rocks jutted out of a seething sea of white mist that seeped across the valley floor and rose up as drifting formless ghosts. The fires on the mountain peaks alternated between leaping, orange flames and a dull angry glow.

The young man spoke for the last time. 'Walk the horror road. Walk the floor of the lowest strata of the underworld, but do not blame me for its conception for you and your kind have created it from guilt and the never ending desire to be punished. Why else should you seek out danger, find an excuse to wage war, then blame the great dreamer when suffering comes pouring down from the sky? But now you can revel in fear, soak your soul in the very essence of danger, shriek with ecstasy-anguish to your heart's content. Should you success-fully reach the red river, retain your sanity when the great monster reaches down to fill its stomach, for then will you acquire power to overcome all fear. We may meet again.'

He fell to the ground, there elongated and took on the form of a golden snake, then glided into oblivion.

I walked forward several steps before the black gates silently closed behind me.

IV

The Underworld

CHAPTER ONE

The underworld was without doubt the end of a black and white rainbow; the never-never-come-back-again-land where fantasy was indisputable fact and the fears one toyed with in an idle moment, was waiting to take on substance. My feet sank into moist, spongy ground and it seemed as if I were walking through a dream. The black and white stillness, the complete absence of sound, plus the exasperating feeling of expending the utmost effort for the slowest possible progress, all contributed to a dream-like quality. When I looked back the gates had disappeared and there only a seemingly endless length of valley, not different to that which lay before me.

After a while I began to take a more careful note of my surroundings and tried to determine their origin and construction. The 'sky' was of particular interest because it could well have been the roof of an immense cave. The 'moon' apart from being extremely large, apparently did not move; was merely a brightly lit globe suspended in a jet-black expanse of space. I decided to think of it as a lamp hanging from a black ceiling.

Then I turned my attention to the mountains. They loomed up on either side, the lower slopes about two hundred yards away, while the average height was about a thousand feet. The ever-flickering flames that lit every peak created a sinister aspect, while widely spaced skeletal trees stood on the lower slopes and even encroached on to the valley floor, rather giving the impression they might break into a macabre dance.

I walked with care, not knowing what pitfall – or worse – might be hidden under the carpet of white mist that in some places whirled around my knees. The further I advanced into the underworld the deeper grew my despair and self-induced confidence seeped away like water from a leaking saucepan. I had no weapon with which to fight off a sudden attack and so

157

far as I could see no suitable materials with which to make any. Neither was there the slightest sign of edible vegetation or game.

But it was not long before the first sign of life put in an appearance. From high up on a mountainside there came the sound of a muted roar followed by a sinister rattling, not unlike that made by an angry rattle-snake. I looked up and saw a nightmare face peering down over a large jutting rock.

It was too far away for me to define the actual features, but there was the impression of two large eyes and some kind of fringe circling a round head. A recurrence of the original roaring sound came from a little way further on, although I had a nasty suspicion it had emerged from another throat. To stand still invited attack; to run, to become first prize in a cross country race. I walked slowly, trying very hard to look unconcerned, not daring to look either left or right.

An hour must have passed and legs began to tire; nerves that had been taut for the past four days, rebelled and I knew I was not far from breaking point. Then I saw the cabin and became as a hungry man who has spotted a well-appointed dining table. It was a very crude affair, built from piled-up rocks and roofed by interlaced tree branches. A dim light flickered inside the hole which served as a doorway and I hurried towards it, spurred on by another muted roar which came from somewhere in my rear.

I stood in the doorway and peered into the interior, quickly noted the lamp which was merely a hollowed out stone filled with some kind of oil; the heap of untanned skins in one corner and the scattered dishes which had been made from baked earth. Then I froze when a sharp object was rammed into my back and a low voice said:

'Move and I'll ram this through your innards.'

I said with a calmness I did not feel. 'I am a wanderer looking for shelter.'

'Yeah! I have to make sure. For all I know you might be a ele-monster on the prowl. Turn round – but slowly.'

With reluctance I obeyed for in this place I had no reason to believe anything even remotely like a human being stood behind me. And what I finally saw was not very encouraging. A short squat man with powerful arms and shoulders, dressed in a tattered leather jerkin, filthy khaki trousers and down-at-heel boots; with long black matted hair and matching beard that all but hid a bulging stomach and small brown eyes that glittered in a most disquieting fashion. The man – if indeed he was – growled:

'You look human enough, but that might be a ruse to catch me off my guard. I'm not supposed to be in one piece now, but I am – and still half sane.'

I wondered if that were even half true but managed to mask my unease under a – hopefully – disarming smile.

'How long have you been in this place?'

'Netjer-Ankh knows. There's no way of measuring time here what with that bloody moon never moving. Maybe a month – maybe a hundred years. Sometimes I think I've never been anywhere else.'

I looked around at the fire-tipped mountains, the mist-haunted valley and remembered the things that roared, then marvelled.

'How on earth do you live?'

'By using me head. Learning to live with terror and telling yourself how exciting it is. You have to here. Swallow terror when you eat, dream terror when you sleep, take it with you when you go for a walk.'

But I could not forget that face that looked down over the jutting rock. 'Do you suppose we could go inside? I saw a dreadful face up there on the mountainside.'

The man grunted. 'Ugle-monnies. Worse faces than that decorate the scenery here. So long as you can move they can't do all that much to you. Unless they get an essence-sucker on you – then give up.'

We went into the tiny stone house and even this frail shelter gave an illusion of security. At least here, so long as one faced the doorway, there was no need to ponder on what might be creeping from the rear and the low roof hid the face of that awful moon. I sat down with my back resting against the far wall and watched my host with something like academic interest.

'How did you come to be here?' he asked.

'A man – that is to say – the Snake God brought me. I haven't any idea where I'm supposed to be going.'

The man closed one eye and widened the other.

'First of all, let's find out who you are and what you're doing here.'

I answered him briefly even though he did not look like anyone that I would like to offend.

'My name is Gore Sinclair and I was sent to the underworld by Princess Helena Landi.'

He spat and glared at me with his one open eye.

'That cow! Cursed by the god. Has snakes for hair! You're in the manure if you've anything to do with her. Me. . .' Now he opened both eyes and his appearance was not greatly improved. 'Me, I'm Marlo Denfire. Sometime or the other I was convicted of corrupting youth. Oh, not what you're thinking. They – the boss class – wouldn't have worried about that. No, I told them the gods were a lot of has-beens. Blasphemy. Almost started a war. So I'm here for ever. Can never cross the red river.'

I swallowed and trembled when I heard a distant roar. 'What is the red river?'

He frowned and his narrow forehead disappeared.

'A river that's red.'

'And if you did cross it. . .?'

'No way. I mean, when you find out what's in it. . .'

'But suppose you did. What's on the other side?'

'Well, since you insist on knowing, here it is. There's the rooted sector, that takes a bit of crossing too, then. . .'

'What happens in the rooted sector?'

'The bloody questions you ask! It's the final barrier before you tackle the ultimate – only of course you never get that far.'

'But the rooted sector. . .?'

'Is a place where you can become rooted, or maybe take root. Any road, you get the general idea?'

Actually I didn't but I nodded just the same and asked:

'Just supposing I get over the red river, cross the rooted sector without taking root, where do I arrive?'

'Pardon?'

'What lies beyond the rooted sector?'

Marlo scratched his head and made a very unpleasant grimace.

'How old are you?'

'Twenty-eight. Why?'

'You mean to tell me you've lived all that time and don't know what lies beyond the rooted sector?'

I sent mental detectors back along the halls of memory, then said ruefully. 'I believe I once knew, but forgot a long time ago. Please tell me.'

He expelled his breath as a vast sigh. 'That cow should never have sent you here. I mean a seepie or a ugle will bring you down before you've gone more than ten yards. Son, beyond the rooted sector lies the land of the gods.'

'You mean. . .?'

'Their happy stamping ground. Mount Olympus, Valhalla, Heaven. Only those that reach it see it as they think it should be. If I make myself clear. But I'm thinking there may be some who never see it at all. An awful lot of faith is needed to wet the cement of reality.'

I thought long, I thought deep before coming up with an astounding decision.

'I think I must reach the land of the gods so that I can accept fear as a friend. That's it – and more.'

Marlo growled deep in his throat and I gradually came to understand that the sound could be translated as laughter.

'Reach the land of the gods! That's rich! In fact it's dripping with richness. You've got a lot of nastiness to get through before you reach the red river.'

But my brain was aflame with excitement and at that moment would have faced any number of monsters, be they material, spectral, earthbound or voices in the night.

'Will you come with me?'

I thought his eyes would leave their sockets and his jaws break so wide did his mouth gape and it took him quite some while before he had regained the power of speech.

'Me? Me even approach the red river banks? Then lurch across the rooted sector . . . to become a bloody great weed? Mister, whoever you are, you're stark raving mad.'

'But surely if we do reach the land of the gods you'll be free. If I can get the princess cured of her curse, then she'll be powerful again and I'll be in favour and I'll see to it you are pardoned and made rich. . .'

Marlo interrupted by waving his hand impatiently.

'Hold it, mister. There's an awful lot of ifs. If we get to the red river, if we manage to cross it, if we don't take root, if the gods don't blast us on sight, if you do what you say you can do. . . It may not be what you might call safe here but at least I'm used to it.'

I jerked my head in the direction of the doorway as a long howling cry came from behind the cabin. 'And you think you'll keep out of their clutches for ever?'

He shrugged. 'Maybe not. Or maybe yes. I've got their measure. Most of 'em run if shouted at. Curse 'em seems to be the answer. Remember this, mister. We're both wandering through a nightmare and in any kind of dream you can stretch the rules to breaking point, only they don't break. You just wake up.'

'But when you enter a nightmare wearing your everyday body, then there's no waking up. Ingenuity is the only answer.'

He nodded towards a long spear that was leaning against one wall.

'Yep. If the worse comes to the worst, I can tickle an ugle in a place he won't fancy, then spit in his eye. They don't go for being spit in the eye.'

'Then it should be easy for you to lead me over the red river and the rooted sector.'

'Oh, come off it! There's something I haven't told you about. The ele-snake. The guardian of the red river. I had a glimpse of it once and I've yet to improve on the speed I put up. And don't ask me to describe it. If there's one fate I fear above all others it's finishing up in that thing's stomach. Still living you understand, still conscious, being slowly digested.'

'That, I agree, would be very nasty. But talking of digesting, what do you eat down here?'

He pointed to three large and three small round basins that stood near a very primitive fireplace. 'I manage. Some of the little horrors that come down from the mountains are quite tasty when boiled down and there's a kind of grey turnip that grows a little higher up that's very nourishing. I won't say my meals are lip-smacking good, but they're filling. A little later we'll go on a hunting and provender picking trip.'

'That will be nice,' I said without any real conviction. 'When's a little later?'

My companion did not answer but sat with his head lowered

and eyes closed. Presently a sound that resembled a saw being driven through a particularly hard piece of wood filled the little hut. Marlo was asleep.

I had almost followed his example when a hideous face peered round the doorway, opened its mouth and roared. I recognized it as belonging to the creature I had seen on the mountainside. I shouted: 'Marlo, Marlo, wake up.'

Marlo came up on his feet and without turning round spluttered:

'What's the matter? Eh? What's the matter?'

Finding difficulty in speaking I pointed to the doorway, whereupon Marlo spun round, gave the head – which emitted another roar – one quick look, then spat upon the floor.

'It's only a bogle for Set's sake. I thought the roof had fallen in.'

I found I was once again capable of making basic sounds.

'But . . . but...'

'But nothing. Get rid of it. They can't stand harsh words. None of 'em can. Damnation! Don't you know anything? Listen.'

And Marlo approached the bogle, stared into the saucer-sized blue eyes, spat on the huge hooked nose and shouted: 'Get out you goggled-eyed-pasty-faced-lump-of-sewer-offal. Get rolling. . .'

Two pint-sized tears ran down the white cheeks as the head gradually withdrew from the doorway. Marlo continued his verbal attack.

'Bum-kisser-pudding-head-tail-wriggler. . .'

With a kind of sobbing roar the head disappeared and Marlo straightened up and wiped his brow. 'Much more of that and I would have lost me voice. Then we'd been in a ripe old state. But you had better have a look at the bogle before it's out of sight. They're a bit off-putting until you get used to them.'

He stood to one side and allowed me an unimpeded view of *what* was swaying towards the mountainside. The head I had already seen, the long neck therefore was just acceptable if one could ignore the large hand which waved its long fingers from a position below the skull. But the shapeless transparent body was quite another matter. It was long – an extension of the neck – and was comprised of some semi-solid material that resembled grey silk. This writhed, contorted, formed two pointed feet that danced over the ground and *appeared* to assist the bogle in its flight. Two minutes of uninterrupted viewing was about all I could take and I withdrew into the hut. Marlo followed and then resumed his former position against the wall.

'Don't let them fool you,' he told me, 'they've got a nasty habit of creeping up behind you, slapping that great hand over yer mouth – then sucking the essence from your body. That's what they feed on, see? When I first came here there was six or seven other fellows doing their time. But now I'm the only one left. All drained. I can remember one bogle that was solid as a house. Bloody great arms and legs – thundering great chest. Used to throw rocks about. All the while crying its eyes out.'

Thus was I entertained by my host and I found it impossible *not* to ask a basic question.

'As I haven't eyes in the back of my head, what do I do to keep alive and in one piece? I mean, those things seem to be able to move without making a sound.'

Marlo grinned. 'Develop an instinct. When you're out in the open let rip with a curse every now and again. I find: "Push off, old misty toes," works wonders. I once heard a shriek from behind and knew I'd missed being sucked in by a single four letter word.' He rose and yawned. 'I suppose we'd better rustle up some fodder. The sooner you learn the ropes, the sooner you'll earn your keep. Then after we've filled our bellies, put in some kipping time, we'll *think* about crossing the red river. *Think* is the operative word.'

I watched him pick up his home-made spear, a long bone honed into a sharp point at one end, then followed him out of the hut and down a slight slope to the mist-covered valley floor. The man raised his bearded face and glared up at the fire-tipped mountains. There was a hint of compressed anger in his voice as he shouted:

'Damned flickering and blazing away up there, reminding a man what might be waiting for him should his essence be sucked dry. But it don't bear thinking about. Just keep living as long as you can.'

We moved cautiously along the valley; past boulders that were designed – for surely there was wind or rain in this place – into weird shapes. Those that stood on the valley floor cast tapering shadows that gave the impression they might at any time leave the parent rock and come dancing after the rash intruder. Marlo glanced back over one shoulder and bared his teeth into a grin.

'Don't do to have a glimmer of imagination in the underworld. There was a time when I did my nut when a flying rat passed overhead, but now I store my anxiety for the big stuff. Bogles, Aldivas, Maggies. There's plenty to really loosen the bowels without worrying about what could be. Now, keep your eyes open for some small life. Pot fodder.'

I looked downward and could only see the milk white mist which hid both of my feet and half of my legs as well: Marlo laughed when he saw my puzzled expression.

'There's plenty of wriggling and sick-making life down below. You'd be surprised as to what's trying to get a grip on your feet this very moment. Most of it boilable, chewable and in the case of the Jullimon, squelchable. Watch.'

Marlo raised his spear, jumped up and down three or four times, then flashed the spear down into the whirling mist.

When he triumphantly raised it again a creature that looked like a deformed jellyfish was squirming on the tip.

'Talking of a jullimon – there is one. Not all that tasty but makes a good thickener. Now I'll try to find something a bit more meatier to join it.'

He again jumped up and down, then drove his spear down and this time came up with a toad-like creature covered with large red eyes. Each eye wept red tears.

'A brothy,' Marlo explained. 'A bit tough and should rightly be baked, but it will help fill the pot.'

During the course of the next hour I had gathered an unappetizing harvest of mushroom-like fungus that Marlo had named Pink-and-grey-'uns, some soggy looking potatoes and bright red carrot-like roots that oozed some evil smelling liquid that I was given to understand would enrich the stew and put hairs on my chest.

Marlo for his part speared several serpent-creatures that snapped viciously until decapitated, two more brothies and several green balls covered with tiny black warts.

Then Marlo cast a quick glance round the bleak scene, kicked something under the mist, then said:

'May as well get back and have a ripe old boil-up. Should do ourselves proud tonight.'

I enquired: 'Tonight?'

He shrugged. 'Well yes. When I feel hungry enough for a big stodge up, that will mean I'm soon due for a longish kip, so that must be night time. Get it?'

I nodded and followed him back into the hut, always being careful where I placed my feet; even so I felt something long and thin wrap itself briefly round my ankle. Once I got a real scare.

Preceded by a sound that was very like a woman's scream, a huge flesh-coloured snake rose up from the mist and revealed it had a parody of a human head on the top end of its plump, pink-tinted body. A head that could have been crudely modelled on that of a young girl. Dark hair, over large deep-blue eyes, a snub nose and clear white skin. I was reminded of someone I had seen somewhere or the other, but I just couldn't remember who or where. Then after another scream (the eyes bulged most horribly) the creature dropped with a sickening thud into the mist and all that kept me upright was the thought that if I fainted I might become entangled with that thing.

Marlo scratched his head. 'Be damned if I've ever seen anything like that before. I mean that head was as near as damn it human. Bit overblown of course, but recognisable. Someone had got in bad with the gods, I guess. Let's get a move on. It may be still lurking around down there and I wouldn't fancy it getting a fix on my foot.'

'Amen,' I agreed with deep sincerity.

Back in the hut Marlo soon lit a fire and I was pleased to notice that the smoke went straight up and out through a small hole in the ceiling; before slicing the various items that he had placed in his bag, then dispatched me to fetch some water in a skin bucket. The water came from a stream that flowed down from the mountains, but I was not made all that happy by the fact it sent off a pungent steam and tasted very strongly of rank earth.

But Marlo was more than satisfied when the contents of a fire-hardened earthenware pot began to bubble and a very unappetizing stench began to fill the hut.

'What did I say? Eh! We'll do ourselves proud. What do you think of me basins?' He took up one small round vessel I had noticed before. 'You'll find some black gourds growing far up the mountains. The contents look like and taste like shit, but when the gourds are cut in half – bloody good basins.'

'Marvellous!' I succeeded in expressing astonishment. 'And those spoons?'

'Gourds again. Carved them to the right shape. We might be in the underworld but there's no need to live in an uncivilized manner.'

To my great horror a long thin snake-thing was sliding over the pot rim, apparently completely unaffected by the boiling liquid from which it had emerged. Marlo swore.

'Those bloody karlleaches never give up. Be careful how you swallow the smallest bit. I've known a three inch length crawl up from the stomach then coil up in the windpipe. Not a nice way to go.'

He levered the repulsive creature back into the pot by means of his spear tip. I registered a formal protest.

'Wouldn't it be better to – well take it out?'

Marlo spat on the floor again. 'Yeah. But if you can keep them down they are nourishing. We've got three of them in there, but don't worry I'll make sure they're well boiled so they'll be tender. But cut 'em up small. And chew well before swallowing.'

There could be no doubt that I was famished for I could not remember when I ate last, but the smell when combined with the knowledge of what was bubbling in that pot, did much to blunt the keen edge of appetite. This was further emphasized when a brothy leaped out of the foul brew and began to bounce towards the door.

Marlo emitted a roar of rage.

'Stop the bloody thing! By Set and Anubis, the entire bloody stew will be prancing up the mountain the way things are going. Use your hands, man. Chuck 'em back in to the pot and I'll ram the lid on. Damn, blast and shag it.'

When I with the greatest reluctance and enormous concentration of courage managed to grip fingers on a brothy, the hideous thing was well nigh red hot, which meant I promptly dropped it. Marlo eventually gathered together the bits and pieces, before covering the pot with a black wooden lid.

A long while later Marlo, not without certain pride, dished out simmering underworld stew – for he had allowed the fire to die down – and when I was presented with a well-filled basin and a carved spoon, not wishing to hurt his feelings even in the slightest degree, forced the hot concoction down my throat and surprisingly found it both pleasant to taste and agreeable to the stomach. Those portions of wriggling karlleaches that I could not ignore were flipped on the floor by my spoon, but all other edible life forms appeared to have been simmered out of any recognizable shape.

I actually lowered two helpings of the savory mess and indeed felt very much the better for them. Marlo rather spoilt the feast by remarking:

'If you do feel a bit of karlleach coming up – let it come. If you try keeping the buggers down they'll only join up with whatever else is floating around and finally force their way out from behind your teeth.'

How I managed to keep anything down after that is beyond me.

Marlo, having swallowed everything that remained in the pot, which included the thick sediment at the bottom, stretched himself out and said: 'Another kip, then we'll think about going to the red river. Yeah, we'll have a good think about that. And I'll sleep on it as well.'

Which he promptly did and I, having decided there was little point in worrying about the various screams and howls that came from all about the hut, also lay down on a pile of smelly skins and fell asleep.

*

When Marlo woke me he was already wearing a large haversack made from reptile skins, the long spear in his right hand, and he did not seem to be in the best of moods.

'Mister, you take some waking up. Won't do here in the underworld. I mean you could be half way down an ele-snake's throat during the time it took me to get you awake.'

I clambered to my feet and instantly began to regret that I had no weapon to defend myself, before Marlo handed me a thick pinkish root which was thin but strong at one end and rounded with spikes at the other, while saying:

'Here you are. A munchem root. Clobber anything with that. Particularly if the clobberee has a soft head.'

With this I had to agree, always supposing I could summons the resolution to strike first.

We set out across the valley floor arriving eventually at a low ridge that enabled us to walk considerably above the mist which was a relief to me, even though I was now plagued by a species of snail equipped with long slimy tails, each with a grey sucker at the very tip which were soon attached to my shoes and trouser bottoms. With a cry of alarm I pointed to these parasites, causing my companion to laugh and state that I must have tender and well washed flesh or the brailles (so apparently they were named) would never have been drawn to me.

'Don't try to pull them off,' he instructed, 'or that thin tail will break and wrigglers will breed under the skin. You want to cut out this washing lark. I've never washed in my life and you won't see any brailles on me.'

'How do I get them off?' I shouted by now in a state of near panic for I had just realised some of the things were up my trouser legs.

'Spit on them. None of the life forms in the underworld can stand spit. Here – for mercy's sake! Let me. You have as much idea of how to spit as I have of laying eggs.'

And he knelt down and began to spit on the small monstrosities, sometimes rubbing saliva on a thin tail, so that they began to drop off on to the rock surface where Marlo was able to kick them into the mist.

By keeping to the ridge we were able to make good progress for the first hour or so, until the valley widened and I saw a forest of black trees covered the mountain slopes on either side and completely blocked the floor so far as the eye could see. Marlo echoed the question that slid across my brain.

'I wonder what's hidden in that little lot?'

'Can we climb the slopes and try to get round it?'

Marlo looked up at the fire mountains.

'It will be a bit warm, but I don't think we have any option.

I'm bloody certain we'd never get through that forest in one piece.'

A concert of howls came from the forest as we started to climb and Marlo's shouted string of curses only increased the din, but thankfully nothing emerged into view. Even so there were many rocks for bogles to hide behind and on one occasion a shriek made me turn on my tracks only to stare into a round white face, just as a great hand was being lowered towards me. I struck out with my club and had the satisfaction of crushing the hooked nose. Marlo watched the screaming monster glide away and said grimly:

'That one almost got you. Keep your wits about you, man. Although when we're a bit higher we should be free of the bastards. None of them can stand fire.'

I had no head for heights and after a period spent in climbing I did not dare look down lest I become giddy and over-balance. The upper fringe of the black forest was only a hundred feet below, but to my horror when we had reached a point that was about mid way between fire-peaks and top-most trees, Marlo stopped and said:

'Hang on to a rock and take a look at the scenery. It will give you some idea of what to expect.'

After much deliberation and the mustering of much depleted courage I gripped a jutting rock and looked out over the valley. The motionless moon high-lighted the scene; made the black trees glitter like dust-grimed tinsel; created islands of ebony shadow and revealed the land which lay beyond.

I estimated the forest was probably three miles long; a solid mass of twisted trunks and leafless branches, without so much as a hand-space between them. In the far distance the valley widened even more, the mountain slopes curved gently down to a long oval basin, which seemed comprised of black meadow land, broken here and there by a twisted tree – and bordered on the right by a broad red river. It began as a lake, then flowed along the valley floor until it disappeared around a far bend. On the far side lay a seemingly unending expanse of growth-covered moorland. From this distance I could not determine what colour or of what nature that growth was.

'There you are,' Marlo said, 'the red river. The home of the ele-snakes.'

'And where does it end?'

'Your guess is as good as mine. Perhaps it never ends. Come on the uglies are watching us from down below.'

An hour later found me crouched in a crevice and sobbing with exhaustion. Marlo, who appeared to be in no way discomforted by the long climb, looked down at me with a smile of contempt.

'You don't seem to have much stamina. If it hadn't been for me, you'd have gone rolling down there long since.'

'I just want a little rest,' I pleaded. 'I'm not used to clambering about on mountains.'

'Rest! That's all you've been doing since we started. I suppose you wouldn't fancy a little climb to the top and find out what makes those flames burn?'

'No, I certainly wouldn't. But I can't help feeling they should be giving out more heat than they do.'

I again looked at the shimmering fires which were now less than a hundred feet above us. Great gouts of orange flame reached up to the black sky, then died down to a hissing glow, before again blossoming into strangely beautiful fiery flowers.

'It is possible,' I said thoughtfully, 'that fire, like everything else here that has a remote claim to animated life, is partly astral. Then fire without heat has a kind of mad logic.'

'But the fire I lit to cook our supper was hot enough,' Marlo pointed out.

'That fire relied on fuel supplied by you. That stuff up there has been created by warped nature. But I don't think we should go any higher, it may well be that the flames give out harmful properties.'

'If it can't burn us, what can it do?'

'Possibly alter our physical structure. Maybe that's why all life forms here are half matter, half something else. Let's get down to the valley as quickly as possible.'

'Fine. But don't forget the red river.'

I again looked up at the fire-crowned peaks. 'Whatever comes out of the river may kill us, but that would be better than never being allowed to die at all. If that happens to me I'll most likely destroy the world.'

'Do you know what you're talking about?' Marlo asked sardonically.

'No. But I have a feeling I soon will.'

The descent was achieved without too much difficulty, for once we had skirted the forest, the mountain sloped gently down to the black meadow land, that in turn formed the banks of the red river.

I drank in the scene, saturated my soul with the weird beauty while I chased elusive memories that refused to be trapped. A velvet sky, a silver moon, a red lake and river, which lapped a black shore. Surely, once long ago, in a different form, in another life, I had visited this strange land before.

I slowly approached the lake, then turned my head and looked down at its lower reaches where the shore curved inward and became the river banks. It was bright-bright red. Thick – as though clotted with undiluted blood – and never still. Rippling gently, disturbed here and there by giant bubbles, reflecting that strange moon which seemed to float just below the surface.

'Don't go too near,' Marlo warned. 'Never know what's going to come out.'

'There's a swift current,' I said thoughtfully, 'and it's flowing down the valley. If we could only make a boat of some kind, we could use the current to get us to the other side.'

Marlo nodded grimly. 'Too true it would. Whatever is in that red soup would have us for breakfast in no time. Come on, let's keep going. Maybe this river does come to an end further along, then we can *think* about crossing over to the other side.'

It was pleasant to walk over smooth ground and I was so fascinated by our surroundings, I almost forgot to be afraid.

The thought came to me: was I really enjoying all this? After all fear is the dark sister of excitement. Marlo's voice broke into my thoughts.

'You're day-dreaming, man. How many times must I tell you to keep alert? Two great bubbles have just formed and burst in the river and I'm pretty sure they weren't caused by a fish.'

'Frankly,' I confessed, 'I've seen so much that is blood-chilling, I'm not all that worried about what could or even might come up from the red river. I cannot believe it can be worse than those bogle things or Madame the Princess's head of snakes.'

Marlo grimaced. ''Ark at 'im! What's so dreadful about head snakes or bogles? The first you keep away from, the second you swear at. The bogles I've kept at bay for longer than I care to remember. Madame the Princess I've never seen, although I've heard about her. Why, by the Black One's toenail, look!'

I turned my head and looked. Something was rising up from the river. It bore some resemblance to a huge flesh snake with a bulging caricature of a human face, but there the comparison ended. I estimated that a fifty feet length of transparent body was rearing up from the river. Fully six feet in circumference, a faint network of veins shimmered like red cotton in a glass tube and curved round in that position where the creature's stomach might be situated. A large bottle-shaped aperture, large enough to hold two men and space to spare.

In fact this premise was amply demonstrated by the vision which caused me to cry out in disbelief.

A man was in the stomach and he was alive. A short, bald-headed man; he was naked and leaning forward so that his nose was flattened as though pressed against glass, his mouth wide open, his eyes pools of madness.

Marlo made the X sign.

'May the gods protect us! The poor sod is in there until fire turns to ice. He feeds the ele-snake and it feeds him. He can never die.'

The ele-snake rose up a further ten feet in height, then began to bend its neck into a graceful curve. I wasted five precious seconds watching the round human-like head coming down towards me, before Marlo shouted:

'Run, man. Run, run . . . *run.*'

I ran. Possibly I never had run so fast before, but there could be no doubt in my mind I was running for something more precious than my life. I was running for the freedom of my soul. If I tripped, allowed my pounding heart a moment's respite, I would never run again.

Marlo, although much stronger than me, was not so fleet of foot, and I became aware he was dropping behind, his rasping breathing growing fainter until it was submerged by a more sinister sound. A kind of bubbling roar that did much to increase the tempo of my pounding feet.

I glanced over one shoulder. The ele-snake was undulating

over the black grass. Mighty humps that rose and fell in graceful curves; the red-lined cavern of a mouth gaping, displaying two rows of pink, toothless gums; it was coming forward at an unbelievable speed. Marlo was now twenty paces behind, his face screwed up into an expression of pain and exhaustion. He gasped:

'I can't go on, man. Help me.'

But the world had shrunk to the limited land of self, whatever strength remained was needed to preserve the frail body of 'I': carry the atom of divinity away from a gaping mouth and the ultimate destination of an oval, transparent stomach.

The red river was shimmering on my right; in front an expanse of black grass land, the towering mountains a row of glowering giants on my left; beyond a sheer slab of grey rock hid the rest of the valley from sight. But the time had come for the body to rebel against the brain's impossible demands; the legs slowed down, the feet stumbled and I fell – crashed down upon the black earth, where I lay praying to the God of my childhood.

'Oh, Lord, let it be Marlo – not me.'

With head pressed down into the coarse grass, like a child trembling under the bedclothes, willing the unseen terror to go away, I enlarged my prayer.

'Lord, let it consume the entire human race, but not me.'

The scream seared my brain and wounded my soul. Hoarse, the agonized cry of a being being drawn in a hell that had been long dreamed about and had now become horrifying fact. Then the scream rose up and lost its hoarse quality, became a high-pitched shriek that made me cover my ears, try to smother it under a blanket of numb conscience; summon the blind forces of forgetfulness, the cringing lackeys of self-excuse.

Not until the shriek was cut off, became low, moaning gurgles, then lapsed into awful silence, was I permitted to uncover my ears, then, fired by an almost obscene curiosity, sit up and look back.

The ele-snake had twisted the lower part of its body round into a neat pile of glistening coils, but the upper half reared up into a straight transparent column: the epitome of beauty blended with indescribable horror, a nightmare that had escaped from the cage of sleep. The head was tilted back and unholy ecstasy glittered in the large blue eyes, the long neck contorted and I was permitted to release a choking cry.

Marlo was sliding down the throat. Hands stretched above his head, hair and beard erect, mouth wide open, kicking with legs that were fast becoming immobilized with thick, green-tinted fluid, clawing with fingers that were streaked with blood.

He finally reached the stomach and was there allowed to take his place beside the little bald-headed man, who greeted the newcomer with bulging eyes, gaping mouth and silent scream. As the ele-snake sank down and so hid the macabre scene from view, I saw that Marlo's clothes were dissolving; melting away into little wisps of grey vapour.

Then a roaring blackness rushed in and for a while, I, Gore Sinclair, gigolo, sometime author, wanderer of the underworld, was lost in the kindly realms of oblivion.

CHAPTER TWO

The black grass was rattling.

I lay perfectly still and gradually allowed my newly returned consciousness to digest this information. There was no wind in the underworld, therefore if the grass was being disturbed, something solid, living and quite possibly lethal was responsible. Then memory rose up from its scarlet nest and reared an accusing head.

I had ignored Marlo's cry for help and in consequence did not deserve to live. Sobs racked my body, loneliness slithered a cold trail across my brain, while grief numbed my senses and relit the lamp of conscience.

Marlo had been my guide, protector, teacher. Now he was a gibbering thing in an ele-snake's stomach, companion to another trapped being, destined to scream until – what had been his expression? – fire had turned to ice.

The grass rattled again. But now the sound was much nearer. I dared to open my eyes and feed insatiable curiosity. For a while I only saw the moonlit valley, the red river, the towering mountains, then, after I had sat up, assured my quivering self that the ele-snake had gone – jerked my head from left to right and saw *it*.

A small creature with a smooth blue body and six transparent legs. The sloping head terminated with a trumpet-shaped mouth; two little green eyes observed me with inquisitive appraisal and a long rat-like tail waved slowly from side to side. When I moved the creature slid back a few inches, then again became still. It made a little croaking sound, but did not display any sign of aggression. I decided it would be safe to speak.

'Be damned if I'm going to be eaten or sucked dry by a little monster like you.'

The thin tail was waved vigorously and the croaking sound

repeated for the space of something like ten seconds. I rose very slowly to my feet, waited until a fit of giddiness had passed, before turning my full attention to the stranger. It was running around in ever-decreasing circles and finally tried to rub its head against my legs. I backed away and aimed a kick at the trumpet-shaped mouth.

'Sheer off. Go jump in the river.'

The thing rolled over on its back and waved all six misty legs, while whipping the ground with the thin tail. A ridiculous notion presented itself for my consideration, but I dismissed it out of hand.

To linger any longer in this place was to say the least extremely dangerous, but I would be courting even greater danger if I carried out my intention of crossing the red river. I knelt down, shielded my eyes with both hands and stared across the crimson rippling surface.

The opposite bank could not be less than a quarter of a mile away, covered so far as I could see with a mass of vegetation that defied identification from this distance, I would have given much for a pair of powerful binoculars. Beyond, partially hidden by a faint golden mist were a range of low hills.

The land of the immortal gods. The Mecca where all problems would be solved and all questions answered.

I looked behind, then all around.

To stay here was to invite eventual disaster – of one kind or another; to cross the river, all but volunteer to join Marlo in the ele-snake's belly. To say nothing of whatever other horrors that lurked, swam or wriggled beneath the rippling surface.

After some while spent in conducting a mental debate, I gradually came to realise that I was wasting time.

Nothing in any world or universe could stop me from at least trying to cross the red river.

The small creature with six misty legs and a trumpet-shaped mouth emitted a series of croaking sounds, then actually did rub its round body against my legs. But I still treated its overtures with grave suspicion, for I could not dismiss the thought it might be softening me up so that I would be easy prey for a pack of little trumpet-mouth horrors, an only slightly less terrifying prospect than being swallowed by an ele-snake.

but even after I had thrown small stones it still continued to follow me.

I dismissed the problem for the time being and instead attempted to find an answer as to how I would cross a river that contained at least one lethal life form. I approached the bank and having knelt down, poked a tentative forefinger into the red liquid.

It was very thick, like tomato juice. I took up a round stone and tossed it into the river. It seemed to be reluctant to sink. I gathered six more small stones and threw them one by one into the thick fluid – and was rewarded – if that is the right word – by the little monster throwing itself into the river and after diving several times, it returned with four stones in its mouth.

Now there could be no doubt – I had got myself an ele-dog.

I even went so far as to pat its hideous head, thereupon it again rolled over on its back, waved its misty legs, tried to lick my hand with a tongue that would have drawn blood, then jumped into the river again. This time it appeared to run over the surface for a few feet before becoming submerged.

The solution as to how I could cross the red river was born as a scarcely acceptable idea. If I were able by some means or the other to make myself two surf boards, I might if blessed by all kindly-intentioned gods and every atom of good luck that had been allocated to me at the beginning of every life, I might reach the other side.

I toyed with the idea. Tossed it across my brain. Bounced it off the wall of commonsense, agreed that such an idea could only have originated from a brain on the verge of total madness.

Then I sat down – with the ele-dog gnawing a grey bone – and began to work out the possible ways and means.

The only material available was the wood from the black, twisted trees that grew on the mountain slopes. But I had no tools to cut down, shape and smooth trees. But of course my damnable brain would insist on remembering that Marlo's spear had a sharp edge and could with patience be utilized as an axe, chisel, plane and even spade. I went looking for it.

This proved to be a terrible journey for the ground which marked the ele-snake's passage was covered with grey slime that had attracted a vast number of mud-coloured worm-like things that at least provided my canine companion with a welcome feast. At last I came across the spear which lay where Marlo had dropped it, together with his game bag.

I was again whipped by lash of conscience when I handled the weapon that had helped defend and feed the ill-fated man during his immeasurable stay in Hellvonia. The bag still held a supply of thinly sliced jullimon sandwiched between thick slabs of brothy, food that unsavoury looking as it was, would keep me going until I found means of providing for myself. The bag also held a knife honed from a length of flint and this I thrust into my waistband; then prepared as I ever would be, set out to acquire surfboard-making material.

The trees proved to be hard as iron and wrongly shaped and I was very near despair until I found a tree which by some means or another had been felled.

Even better, owing possibly to termites or whatever was their equivalent in Hellvonia, the centre had acquired a hollow that was more than large enough to accommodate me and whatever I took with me.

My ele-dog raised three transparent legs and christened the proposed ship of discovery. After some thought I came up with a name that I considered to be rather apt, *Blood Vessel*, as the stuff which flowed between the banks looked like, smelt like, and I have no doubt tasted like blood.

This ready made craft needed a little trimming here and there, the loose shavings and wood dust scooped out, then dragged down to the river edge. It floated on an even keel and when equipped with two paddles – fallen branches from another tree – I could think of no reason why – with enormous good fortune – I should not make a safe journey to the opposite bank.

I looked at the creature who had adopted me and decided that there was no way I could leave him behind. The result no doubt of our built-in infatuation for any smallish creature that demands our hospitality. I placed Marlo's bag, spear and knife into my boat, motioned the ele-dog to jump aboard – which it promptly did – then seated myself in the centre and began to ply the paddles.

The liquid was so thick I had extreme difficulty in making any headway, also the stench that came from every side was enough to make me sick. Not so the ele-dog who leaned over the side and lapped the stuff up with every sign of satisfaction. After about an hour I found myself in mid-river alive to the fact that certain under-water creatures were displaying an unwelcome attention in me and my craft; round bullet-hard heads rose up and bumped the vessel, whip-thin tails swished through the air and on one occasion narrowly missed cutting my cheek to the bone.

The ele-dog became very excited when faced by these visitors and croaked rapidly and with deep feeling; it actually grabbed one by its pointed nose and dragged it aboard. Only by skewering the wriggling body on the tip of Marlo's spear was I able to dispose of it again.

It was hot out there on the red river due to the temperature of the fluid which in places sent up little spirals of steam. Also the current was much stronger at the half way point and I had to double my paddling effort, which did not stop me being carried slowly sideways.

Fido – so I had named the ele-dog – became very excited and kept up an incessant croaking, while staring at me with evident anxiety, an emotion I shared with him, for despite my frantic paddling I soon realised my frail craft was being forced into the lake.

Lake suggests a roughly circular pool of water of any size from an over large puddle to an inland sea. The red lake was oval-shaped, was possibly half a mile across its widest part, the banks above the topmost section covered with nest-like growths that seemed comprised of grey bramwells. The liquid here was of a brighter colour than in the river, suggesting freshly shed blood and the continuous bubbling was rather alarming.

The *Blood Vessel* began to spin round and no amount of paddling on my part could bring it back under control; this continued until I found myself in the very centre of the lake where without moving in any direction I was gently rocked from side to side. Fido crouched back on four legs and attempted to cover his eyes with the other two, but, as they were transparent, he was not very successful.

I sank back in the stern and waited for something to happen. Under the circumstances there was not much else I could do.

The ele-snake rose up from a few yards to my left, red liquid pouring from its grotesque head and upper body; two-thirds at least was hidden under the lake – including the transparent stomach.

I was much closer to it than on the first occasion and I could not run away or dismiss the monster from my mind. Also I had more than used up my ration of fear and now I just wanted to get whatever was going to happen over as quickly as possible. Otherwise body and brain were numb, beyond the realms of pain or fear and I even wondered in a whimsical sort of way if there would be room for me in the ele-snake's stomach.

Then it reared even higher, bringing more of its body up from the lake until the transparent stomach was at last revealed.

I could not dismiss what I saw from my mind, I could not run away, but I was just capable of closing my eyes. I closed them.

The boat continued to rock gently, Fido groaned softly, various swimming life snapped, bumped, flicked with whip-like tail, but one sound stood out from all others.

A whining, thin-thread of a voice that pleaded: 'Help me.'

I had to open my eyes and look upon the naked face of truth.

The ele-snake was about to perform its graceful curve, which meant its transparent stomach was immediately to my front, the two naked men standing side by side, mouths gaping, eyes appealing, only now I could hear the familiar voice of Marlo.

'Help me, you yellow bastard, help me. . .'

And I knew the only way I could help him and I only had a few seconds in which to perform the act of mercy, I who could not kill a snail, boil a live lobster, watch an eel cut up on a fishmonger's slab.

I took up Marlo's spear, grabbed the shaft in both hands, then thrust it with all my strength into the ele-snake's stomach, into the heart of Marlo, whose muted terminal scream was over laid by the monstrous roar that came from his gigantic host.

Now something like a tidal wave sent the *Blood Vessel* hurtling back towards the river; made Fido leap into the thick turbulent liquid and me grip the boat side with every last atom of my strength, determined to sink or float with my miserable craft, for I could do nothing more than watch a swaying monster, while in its stomach a screaming bald man clawed at the beard of a dead man.

The miniature tidal wave took the boat on its breast and bore it away and a dying ele-snake roared a death dirge as it sank down into the lake, thus providing some kind of tomb for Marlo and his unknown companion. Not that I assumed he would remain in one piece for long.

I took up the paddles again and began to direct the boat towards the far shore and although I lost half of one paddle to a pair of snapping jaws, I managed eventually to beach my craft on to a beach of black mud and wade across it to more firmer ground. A loud croaking sound informed me that Fido had swum safely ashore and as though to emphasise this fact the ele-dog began to rub his head against my mud-caked trousers, then run back to the water line from where – to my great disgust – he returned carrying a squirming creature that seemed to be half snake, half fish.

I walked forward a dozen yards or more until I came to the expanse of vegetation that I had first seen from the opposite side of the river; I stopped and forced my brain to accept the scene that stretched out before me.

Marlo had called it the rooted sector.

The plants – trees – semi-man-semi-something. A plantation of red-haired men. Only there was only one man duplicated over and over again. Hair-covered torso, arms, legs, face and head. But the legs merged with something that could have been a young tree trunk. Little ones nestling between giant ones, or sheltered by medium sized ones; tiny seedlings with minute red-hair heads that could hardly be seen. A single strand of red hair peeping through disturbed soil. And this awful plantation stretched out before and on either side, nourished no doubt by the red river when it overflowed its banks. The tallest 'Plant' was around five foot high and these raised their hair-matted arms while from their gaping mouths there came a moaning wail such as one might expect from more mundane vegetation when tormented by a strong wind.

Fido inspected several of these rooted beings, watered two which seemed to distress them for their wailing rose to a higher pitch, while their arms flailed like the vanes of a windmill caught in a cross-wind.

Alive with curiosity I approached one fully grown plant-man (what else could I call them?) and stared into its eyes. They were large and blue, but without a gleam that would denote intelligence, but rather like those of a suffering animal.

I asked: 'Can you understand me? Can I help you in any way?'

All I got was an unblinking blank stare and the moaning if possible became more pronounced. A surprisingly well-shaped hand tried to clutch my arm, but there was little strength and I easily pulled it free. Hellvonia as I had reason to know, was a place where horror shrieked from a blank wall, but nothing I had seen so far exceeded the pathetic terror that chilled my very soul as this phenomenon of a man with at least ten thousand heads and unnumbered roots.

I looked down at Fido who promptly wagged his tail while emitting a salvo of croaks. 'Well, old son, we've got to find a way through this lot before we can come to the land of the gods. I wonder which one is responsible for this poor fellow's predicament?'

Fido set an example by streaking through quivering trunks, pausing now and again to sniff at wailing undergrowth, or irrigate a moaning sapling, then lose himself in this grotesque forest, there to croak plaintively until I called him to me.

And me? I adjusted – as always. Every head, irrespective of size, looked alike. If this was an example of retribution, then what sins had this red-haired man committed to be thus tormented? Or more likely – what god had he offended and would he ever be granted absolution?

I walked between wailing misery and rejoiced that I so far – so far – had not been cursed in like manner, but then found that I had reason to be cautious, placate the spectre of panic, walk the floor of Hellvonia with lowered head.

Fido had raced ahead, as usual croaking loudly and I had almost forgotten his existence for I was certain that my journey through the underworld was almost complete, when the ele-dog replaced joyous croaking by a high-pitched whistling sound. It was as near to howling as the strange creature could produce and I instantly broke into a run, wove a trail in and out of trunks, calling out 'Fido . . . Fido. . .' until I came to a very large clearing.

Fido was being pulled into a shallow pit of loose soil by a pair of red-hair-covered hands.

They were the size of those one might expect on a fourteen

year boy, visible from the wrists downward, the finger nails long, slightly curved and bright pink. Whatever they were attached to under the soil must have been endowed with extraordinary strength, for Fido was being dragged down into the hole despite the combined efforts of his six legs and the tenuous grip that his teeth had acquired on a small trunk.

I did not hesitate; I put the point of Marlo's spear on that point where the wrist joins the hand and pushed it down with all my strength. The result was hair-raising.

Every head, large, medium or small, screamed in unison. Ten thousand plus heads with one voice. And Fido broke free and at once began to scratch into the loose earth thereby exposing a seemingly endless root shaped like a human arm. But the thought which all but paralysed me was: if Fido had not run ahead and got himself trapped, it would have been me fighting to pull myself free from two earth-based hands.

From then on I walked slowly and with great care, prodding the ground with my spear before taking the next step. Fido slunk in my footsteps.

When I stepped past the furthermost man-plant the continuous lament ceased as though with my departure, whatever hope my presence had generated, expired. When I looked back all I could see was the back of heads and necks of a crop of red-haired men. All faces were turned from me.

Ahead lay a range of low hills, their peaks gleaming like polished silver in the moonlight.

I had arrived in the land of the immortal gods.

CHAPTER THREE

Lush blue grass intermingled with scarlet blooms. Trees adorned with sweet smelling blossom. A stream of crystal clear water that tasted like smooth sweet wine. Fido drank an inordinate amount and did not walk straight for a long time. The moon had become very bright and looked as if it might turn into a sun at any moment, even while it tinted a stationary cloud bank a gentle pink. A small grotto formed from pink rock was equipped with a silver spout from which flowed a continuous stream of cool milk: further on fresh honey bubbled up into a white marble basin.

The immortal gods – irrespective of nationality – did themselves proud.

Fido and I – admittedly travel-worn – arrived at the lower slopes of Celestial Mountains. They might in fact have only been hills, but when one remembered who existed among them, Mountains (with a capital M)) seemed to be the correct definition.

Presently we came to a golden path into which had been embedded every kind and size of precious stone that the imagination can conceive or the eye witness. After a gentle incline that elevated but did not tire, we came to an immense bronze door set in the mountainside. Fido croaked three times – and the door glided open to reveal a huge hall that appeared to have been hewn from solid rock. About half way along the left hand side was another door, a much smaller one made from silver. Fido, without hesitation, ran to this portal and croaked six times. I – not to be out-done by a mere ele-dog – walked boldly up to the silver door and turned the crystal handle – then pushed.

Three steps took me into the presence of the immortal gods.

They were all seated round a long boardroom table and wore black jackets and pin-striped trousers. The one with brushed

back white hair I knew to be Zeus-Odin – mighty father of the
gods – he sat in an immense armchair at the very head of the
table. On his right was the beautiful young man who had led
me into the underworld. Netjer-Ankh, the Snake God.

It was he who welcomed me.

'Greetings, dear boy,' he said. 'Welcome to Olympus and all
stations south.'

*

They had their faces turned in my direction and I did not even
try to identify each one, even if that had been possible. The
Snake God first bowed to Zeus, then smiled at me.

'Please take a seat at the bottom of the table. Our revered
chairman has reserved it for you. Once you have made yourself
comfortable we will get down to the business on hand. The test
which will decide if my curse be lifted from Princess Asherian,
or if she continues to endure my displeasure for a few more
centuries. For I am certain if you fail no one else will succeed for
a very long time – if ever.'

A murmur of agreement flowed down the table and Zeus said
in a deep sonorous voice. 'He's been the most promising one so
far.'

The Snake God nodded his agreement, then as though
remembering protocol, bowed low to the king of the gods.

'I am indebted, sire for your opinion, yet if he cannot
embrace Asherian, clasp her head to his naked bosom, then, sir,
he is not for us.'

Zeus assumed a tiny frown and I could sense a tremor run
down the assembled gods, causing many a divine back to
shiver. His voice was a little like thunder heard from a long way
off when he spoke.

'We are well aware of the details of this case, Netjer, but I
would like to hear the opinion of the young mortal who has
travelled so far to be with us. You have our permission to speak,
young man.'

I spoke boldly for having endured much in the past few days
I had lost much of my respect for high authority.

'In my opinion her offence did not warrant the terrible curse
that Netjer-Ankh placed upon her. A temporary infatuation for
a pretty face. She would have soon tired of him. After all, you –

as befitted a god – must have had your – your worshippers.'

The Snake God frowned but gave a reasonable answer.

'It is natural for a teapot to be surrounded by any number of tea-cups, but it is most unseemly for one tea-cup to be surrounded by more than one teapot.'

A murmur of agreement drifted along the table and I noticed that Zeus nodded most vigorously. I permitted myself a pale smile.

'I couldn't agree more, but I still maintain that the punishment out-ranks the crime. Then there is the matter of the girl Fiona. Her essence absorbed by a flesh snake. . .'

Zeus quickly interrupted. 'It ill becomes you to criticise the immortal gods. The human race have never been more than toys on our nursery floor. As those toys were made for us, surely we have the right to knock them around. If it so pleases us.'

'But surely the essence of power is compassion?' I said sententiously.

Now the murmur that ran down the table was an expression of astonishment. The Snake God spoke for all.

'Where on earth did you get that idea from? The essence of power is power. So long as we can marry the word duty to any one of our acts, there's no limit to the damage we can do. But,' he laid a hand on my arm and I tried not to tremble, 'you have not come here at considerable risk to yourself to bandy words with us. You have been permitted to enter our presence to undergo a final test. History will testify we are very good at setting tests and only either demi-gods or rash heroes ever passed them. So . . . I would suggest there be no more word play, that in fact we summon the former Princess Asherian to appear before us and undergo the test which will either set her free, or,' all heads were turned in my direction and every face wore an anticipatory smile, 'she be given another afflicted companion to accompany her through the centuries.'

'With a great hate to keep them warm,' Zeus murmured. He looked round the table. 'Anyone care to second that? We might as well do the business properly.'

A very shapely young woman with a straight nose and a marvellous jaw line raised her right hand.

Zeus gave her a lecherous smile. 'Very well, Venus, it will be so recorded. Summon the former Princess Asherian.'

No voice disturbed the silence which had suddenly closed down on that long room and I found myself examining the portraits that lined both walls; all depicting persons of both sexes remarkable for their lack of clothing: the men were mostly well-muscled and the women amply fleshed. The Snake God noticed my interest and whispered: 'Tastes change, we've all lost a great deal since those were painted.'

A door at the end of the room opened and Madame the Princess entered the room. She was covered from head to foot by a white sheet that made her look like the conventional idea of a shrouded ghost. She walked to a spot about mid-way along the table, there stopped and bowed her head as though in submission. The voice of Zeus had something in common with thunder heard from a long way off on a summer afternoon.

'You were formerly the Princess Asherian? The beloved of Netjer-Ankh, Lord of Snakes?'

Her voice sounded muffled. 'I am.'

'And you are willing to place your future in the hands of a male wanton who sold his favours in the market place and has never given or accepted love from either man or woman.'

'I am.'

'Knowing that if he shrinks from you and cannot embrace with joy what you have become, then the curse will remain with you *both* for all eternity?'

'That I know.'

'Then let the mortal stand forth so that the trial may be judged.'

The Snake God turned his head and I saw that his face was now lean and grey and his eyes a cold amber stare; his sibilant voice whispered:

'Go and work your miracle and prove to this august assembly that water can be drawn from a dry well and fruit grow on a barren tree. Go and look upon a body from which the gift of beauty has been withdrawn and replaced by the grotesque, then clasp her head to your naked bosom.'

I rose and walked round the table until I stood opposite the shrouded figure of Madame the Princess. The Snake God hissed an order: 'Remove the shroud.'

At first some alien emotion would not allow me to raise my hands, but when for the third time I heard a murmur drift along the table, fear flared up – then was extinguished by pure all-consuming power-knowledge. I used both hands to remove the white sheet, then having dropped it to the floor accepted the wisdom that can only be whispered by Truth, the only goddess that can never be deceived.

The princess's white haggard face was now framed by long writhing flesh-coloured snakes with pink heads. At the back they hung down to a little below her shoulders. There was also three short stubby ones under the left breast and one under the right. Not less than six red boil-like protuberances were situated on and just above the stomach; one ripe and close to eruption stood out on the left hip. All the snakes appeared to be fully aroused; tongues flickering, necks arched.

My thoughts were straying down a shadow haunted road; the roaring waves of eternity were flung on to the beach of memory, the sudden surge of power and knowledge made my head spin.

Then I looked into the dark eyes of the princess and released a laugh of pure joy. I called out without turning my head.

'Summon Katrina.'

I heard the Snake God push back his chair; his voice took on a deeper tone.

'That creature has no place here.'

I raised my voice to a higher pitch. 'I summon Katrina. Let her stand side by side with her alter ego.'

The Snake God was now beside me, his amber reptillian eyes glaring into mine. 'She is not an alter ego, only an image the princess created for her own amusement.'

I shook my head. 'In the beginning, yes, but the image fed from its creator. I demand that she stand beside the princess.'

A united cry of protest rose up from the divine board.

'Demand?'

'Demand. Have I not walked the length of Hellvonia? Did I not kill the ele-snake, cross the red river. Walked free from the rooted sector. Can you deny me a place among yourselves?'

Zeus could have been carved from stone, then given a voice that created echoes in high places. 'You are claiming godhood?'

'Not claiming – assuming it. Zeus, long ago you took memory from me, then banished me from the divine family. Now I have passed the test – memory and power have returned. I am . . . I am. . .'

The king of the gods covered his face with his wide-spread

hands while the others – all – backed away and took refuge on the opposite of the table. I raised a hand and they all became as marble statues. My voice echoed along the avenues of space-time.

'Let Katrina stand by the Princess Asherian. I so order.'

The snakes became still when the princess lowered her head.

Katrina entered the room from the far doorway and very slowly walked to Madame the Princess and there stood facing me; she was again wearing the white muslin dress and her glorious red hair tied into a pony tail with a matching ribbon. I again raised my voice and it seemed as if I was acting out a role that had been mine since the dawn of time.

'Remove the dress.'

Her hands were twin white birds that flew to her neck and bosom and the dress lay like a wind-rippled pool at her feet.

I again called out. 'Helena-Asherian, one time lady of the shrines, come to me if you would be free of the curse of the Snake God.'

For a while nothing happened, then Katrina walked towards me, and I tearing the shirt from my breast, fearlessly took her into my arms and pressed her head to my naked flesh. When I looked up the creature covered with flesh-snakes had disappeared.

Then I deigned to explain. 'Have not the immortal gods learned that eternal is a meaningless word? No thing, no being remains unchanged. When you cursed Asherian her body and mind began to evolve so as to negate an unnatural state of being. Snakes were never intended to grow on a human originated body. Finding she could not free the original body, she sub-consciously began to create a new one. But the old or original princess also realised that she would be soon replaced by the new one and so began to hate and fear it without actually knowing why.

'Lords of the thirty-seven universes, Madame the Princess Asherian-Helena-Landi is free from the curse of the Snake God and now re-assumes the powers and gifts that were long ago granted to her.

'At the same time I re-assume the powers and privileges of my godhood and warn you all, let no one attempt to deprive me of them again.'

Zeus displayed distinct signs of becoming extremely agitated.

'But you had to be put down. My father Cronus had no business in calling you up in the first place. Damn it all, we can manage quite well without a god of destruction. And when you even went so far as to threaten me. . .'

Katrina-Asherian and I stole off together and created our own Olympus.

*

Well, gentlemen, that's about it. Don't try to have me committed to the local lunatic asylum for I really am the god of destruction. That means I have the power to destroy anything or anyone whenever I feel like it. I'm not a vindictive god, but you must try to see my point of view. When you've got power sooner or later you just can't control the urge to use it.

Now this so called civilization . . . well I'm sorry, but I think it stinks and I find myself imagining what it would be like if I wiped this planet clean of all so called intelligent life and started all over again.

I mean, well, wouldn't an evolved reptile be more satisfactory than the offspring of a quarrelsome tribe of monkeys. I mean, did you know the dinosaur was supposed to have made it last time round? Only a nasty inter-galaxy accident stopped a nice little relation of the big boys from mounting the Earthian throne.

And, gentlemen, I know myself, one day quite soon I'll let rip on all cylinders and wham – goodbye to you lot.

Look, I'm an immortal god, but if you fellows – all of you, no matter what race, colour or breed – were to pool all your resources, well, just maybe you'll be able to put paid to me. Old Zeus was able to do it last time. But you'll have to put a move on.

Frankly I don't give a lot for your chances, but while I'm still able to I did think you should be given a sporting chance of saving your own bacon. Katrina agrees with me.

Well if you think I'm mad, good luck to you, but in the name of self-preservation don't even think of laying rude hands on me, for I won't be able. . . .